Praise for Shelly Laurenston's *Pack Challenge*

5 Angels and *FAR Recommended Read!* "Pack Challenge by Shelly Laurenston is a remarkably entertaining page-turner that I took great pleasure in reading. There were moments where I was bowing over with laughter and then in the very next, I was left breathless with luscious anticipation. ...Everything from the humorous moments to sensational passion in Pack Challenge will be forever etched in my mind. This is a must-read!" ~ *Contessa, Fallen Angel Reviews*

5 Tattoos! "An alpha bitch with a temper to match, Sara turns out to be the last woman you want to mess with. Unless of course you're an Alpha male due to become pack leader any day now and just as ornery as your new mate. ...I always knew some of the best encounters happen when both partners can still smile and have fun while blowing each other's socks off. ...the riveting plot kept me on the edge of my seat, excited the entire time about what could happen next and how great the nex⋯ ⋯n scene would be." ~ *Desiree Farrell, Erotic-Escapades*

Pack Challenge

Shelly Laurenston

A SAMHAIN PUBLISHING, LTD. publication.

Samhain Publishing, Ltd.
2932 Ross Clark Circle, #384
Dothan, AL 36301
www.samhainpublishing.com

This book has been previously published.
First Samhain Publishing, Ltd. electronic publication: July 2006
First Samhain Publishing, Ltd. print publication: October 2006

Dedication

To my Maxie. A meaner, nastier Alpha Male I've never known. But you protect me and, as long as I remember to feed you, you love me. Besides, when you're muzzled, you're damn near civilized.

Meet Shelly Laurenston

Subtle, demure, delicate Shelly Laurenston is a 2005 EPPIE Award Winner and 2004 CAPA Winner.

A misplaced New Yorker trapped in Los Angeles, Shelly is constantly plotting and scheming her way back to civilization—think "Escape From New York." When she isn't playing video games, polishing her brass knuckles, or writing, she's trying to keep her dog, Maximus Psychotixus, from turning the local cat population into Happy Meals.

www.shellylaurenston.com

shelly_laurenston@earthlink.net

http://groups.yahoo.com/group/shellylaurenston

Look for these titles from Shelly and Samhain Publishing…

The Distressing Damsel in PRINT! ~ *August 2006*

Go Fetch ~ *March 2007*

Prologue

Waste of his time. That's what this was. Minutes of his life he would never get back. Zach walked into the club, surprised to find a place like this, called Skelly's, in this dinky little Texas town. Hardcore industrial and tech music tore through the tiny building and Zach let himself relax a little. Based on the outside of the club and all the pickup trucks in the parking lot, he assumed this place would be redneck heaven. His kind usually ended up in the middle of a shit storm around rednecks. Too much testosterone and liquor always led to trouble.

He moved through the tightly packed club, checking out everyone, until he reached the bar. He watched the bartender, a cute, petite black woman with a shaggy mass of dark curly hair, pull drinks for a few moments. She was definitely a pro and each drink she made absolutely precise. She never gave any more or less than necessary. Plus, she kept up a continuous conversation with a tall, seriously hot Latina at the other end of the bar and never missed a beat. Never splashed a drop. She was good.

He held up a ten and the bartender moved down to him. He caught the last bit she yelled to her friend, "I can't watch her and serve. I thought you were watching her." She turned to Zach and flashed him an adorable smile. "What'cha need?"

"Tequila."

The girl nodded and her hand went searching under the bar, then her face froze. She suddenly disappeared, crouching low to get a closer look. "Motherfucker!" she snapped. When she re-appeared, she'd lost her smile. "Gimme a sec." She headed to a door behind her, yelling over at the Latina, "Angelina, she took the bottle."

"Uh-oh." The Latina turned and looked out across the dance floor to a group of tables and barstools filled with people. Zach followed the woman's line of sight and immediately saw her.

She was tall; taller than her concerned friend. Her coal-black hair reaching past her shoulders and brushing across the strap of her black tank top, which showed off the Celtic tattoo on her right shoulder. When she turned her head, Zach could clearly see the ragged scar that tore across one side of her face.

Surrounded by four young men, she didn't seem to notice them. In fact, she seemed downright bored. He wasn't quite clear what her friends were worried about.

"Here ya go." The bartender pushed the shot of tequila in front of him. "Your change."

Zach waved it away. "Keep it."

"Thanks." She shoved the cash into the back pocket of her jeans and returned to the end of the bar to speak to her friend.

"Well, we've got to do something," she said. Zach could hear her over the music and even the words she spoke with her back to him came in crystal clear. "She's toasted."

"Yeah, but remember what happened last time? I guess we should just be grateful she doesn't drink every day...or year. Or decade."

"What's with her tonight anyway?"

"I think her leg's been bothering her."

"Her leg is always bothering her. What makes this new?"

"It's getting worse. And I think she's worried. Worried what it might mean."

"It doesn't mean shit. She reads too much into stuff."

The dark-haired beauty leaned back and stared at her friend. "Look who's talking. Pot, this is kettle calling."

The girl flipped the bird and deftly made a martini all in one move. He was impressed.

"Uh-oh, Miki. She's on the move."

Zach turned back to the other girl. She slipped off the stool she'd been perched on and in the middle of some guy's sentence simply walked away. Well, more like she limped away, but he'd heard her leg had been severely damaged. Still, she used no cane or crutches as she, most likely, made her way to the bathroom.

He wouldn't have thought another second about the whole thing except for the two men leaning against a far wall. They didn't fit in, although they were desperately trying to. They wore black leather jackets, but brand new ones that looked as if they'd been bought that day. Their shirts were black, but silk. The pants pleated. And their shoes? They were leather, expensive, and Zach wouldn't put those fucking things on his feet if there was a gun to his head. And as soon as she moved, they followed. Zach shot back his tequila then followed them all.

He'd just pushed his way through the crowd and to the back of the club when he spotted them. One grabbed the girl around the waist, lifting her off the ground. He slapped a hand over her mouth and the three of them were out the back door. It happened so fast none of the other patrons even noticed.

Zach burst into a run, knocking people out of his way, terrified he might be too late. He slammed through the back exit and spilled out into the alley.

They'd thrown the girl down on the ground and one had his hand raised above her. To anyone else it would have looked as if he were going to slap her. But Zach knew one swipe from that hand would rip the girl's throat out. He snarled, forcing his canines to lengthen and grow. The two men turned and one roared in answer.

But before Zach could make any kind of move, the girl pulled a long, thin piece of metal out of her worn cowboy boot and stabbed up into the inside thigh of one of her attackers. He roared again, this time in rage and pain. The unharmed one seemed to realize this was no longer a simple plan of killing the girl. She wasn't going to die quietly. So he grabbed his partner and the two sprinted from the alley, leaving a trail of blood behind.

Zach went over to the girl who, by now, had slipped the weapon back into her boot and attempted to pick herself up off the ground—clearly a major chore. Zach sighed and grabbed her arm, easily hauling her up.

"Hey!" she snapped, looking up at him. From where he sat at the bar, he hadn't realized exactly how pretty she was. Amazingly pretty. Dark brown eyes peered at him from under black lashes. Her skin a light brown, with a hint of red. And the brutal scar on one side of her face couldn't hide her sharp cheekbones or full lips. In fact, it only enhanced them.

Those intense eyes stared straight at him. "Pretty teeth," she drunkenly mumbled. She had a light Texan accent. Not as hearty as the others he'd heard on his ride from California. "Long." Her right index finger slid inside his mouth. It suddenly occurred to him he hadn't yet retracted his canines.

Smiling at him, she said, "You're pretty, too." Wow, she was *really* drunk. With a sudden surge of strength, she slammed Zach against the far alley wall. "I've never seen anyone as pretty as you."

Zach had been called a lot of things in his lifetime, "pretty" wasn't one of them. Growling as she smiled—uh, no—*leered* at him while her body leaned into his, her T-shirt–covered breasts pushed into his chest, startling him with the heat of her body.

She kissed him. Soft lips on his mouth; tongue sliding past his teeth.

Their tongues connected and Zach had this incredible urge to take her right there, in the alley. When he felt her hand slide down the front of his jeans and take firm hold of the bulge growing by the second, he knew he had to have this woman. Now. This minute. This very moment. Before he could even put his arms around her, though, they pulled her from him. Torn, was how he thought of it.

He'd been so lost to her he didn't even realize her friends had burst into the alley, clearly prepared for a fight. The one called Miki had a baseball bat, probably from behind the bar. The other, Angelina, had removed her high-heeled shoes and seemed ready to handle the situation with her bare hands. Yeah, those designer clothes didn't fool Zach for a second. That woman would cut your throat as soon as look at you. She definitely had that take-care-of-herself quality.

"Sara!" Angelina yelped while yanking Sara back from Zach. Miki stood back and stared, the bat still at the ready. Zach could only imagine how it must look to them with their friend's tongue down a stranger's throat and her hand on his crotch. "What are you doing?"

Zach quickly retracted his canines back to normal human incisors seconds before Angelina looked at him, carefully sizing him up. Shame he couldn't control his dick the same way he did his teeth.

Sara pulled away from Angelina and leaned back into Zach. She smiled again, her eyes on his lips. "This is my pretty man. Isn't he great? I think I love him."

Miki rolled her eyes and lowered the bat. "You have got to be kidding me."

Angelina moved toward her friend. "Okay, honey, that's the half-bottle of tequila talking. Now it's time to let the 'pretty man' go."

"No!" she snapped, causing her friend to stop in her tracks. Zach watched, startled at Sara's level of aggression.

But her friends seemed completely unaware of how close they were to real danger. Miki burst out laughing while Angelina looked more annoyed. "Sara, honey, you've got to let your toy go."

"Hey," Zach growled.

Angelina glared at him. "Work with me," she bit out between clenched teeth.

"Okay. Okay." Sara straightened up. "Don't fight on my account. I can take a hint. I'll go."

Angelina visibly relaxed. "Good."

"But first…" Sara whispered so only Zach could hear, her hand slipping around the back of his neck and pulling him down so their faces were barely an inch apart. "It would be just rude not to say night."

She kissed him one more time. And that urge to take her returned full force, whether her friends were watching or not.

"Whoa!" Miki exclaimed with a laugh.

Before he could slam Sara face down over a garbage can, Angelina had her friend by the waist, dragging her back to the club. "Come on, sassy girl. We need to get some coffee into you before you set somebody's car on fire…again."

"Bye-bye, pretty man." Sara waved at Zach.

Miki pulled the back door open as Angelina, literally, threw her friend inside. "That's it. No more tequila for you, missy. Ever."

Miki followed them but stopped at the entrance. She turned and looked at Zach. "Sorry 'bout that. She's really drunk."

"No problem," Zach forced out, using all his inner strength to simply control his dick.

Miki flashed a pretty smile and turned to enter the club. She stopped short. "Jesus Christ, Angie! Get her off the floor!"

Zach pulled out a cell phone and pushed a button. While he waited for the connection, he quickly adjusted his suddenly tight-fitting jeans. "Hey," he answered when he got a pick up. "It's Zach. It's definitely her. But they're already here."

Chapter One

"He's on the List."

"But he just—"

"He's on the List."

Sara sat behind the counter of Marrec's Choppers, the store she'd worked at since she was fourteen, and watched the now weekly ritual between her two best friends.

"Sara," Miki demanded. "The List."

"Would you two bitches please stop. I have a migraine."

"No. You have a hangover. Now, the List."

Sara sighed. "No cowboys. No bikers. No criminals of any kind. And no republicans."

"And?" Miki pushed.

Sara and Angelina shrugged.

"No rodeo clowns."

"You just added that," Angie snapped. A rodeo clown asked her on a date that very morning.

"No. No. They were always on the List."

"He's a nice guy."

"He dodges bulls for a living. He's gonna screw you over!"

"Stop yelling." Sara put her head in her hands. "Just let me die in peace."

"That's what you get for getting all liquored up," Miki chastised.

Angie slipped an arm around Sara's shoulders. "Honey, it's been six months since your grandmother died. Maybe it's time to stop celebrating. Especially since you seem to become quite the whore when you drink."

"I do not." Yet Sara couldn't help but smile at the faint, drunken memory of attacking some poor guy in the alley of her favorite club. "Besides, I'm not celebrating. I'm just glad that my grandmother's—"

"In hell?" Miki cut in.

"There's no proof of that." Especially since Sara felt pretty confident Satan wouldn't take the vicious old heifer.

Sara rubbed her temples. The pain in her head would go away eventually. Besides, pain had always been part of her life. That would never change. Her right leg had been in varying states of unbearable pain for more than twenty years. She'd simply learned to ignore it. Until lately. Lately it had been...no. She would not start feeling sorry for herself. That was what led to the drinking the night before. Stupid self-pity. Her life could definitely be worse. Hell, she could be dead.

Or, she could be like the girl stumbling through the front door of the shop, her face and biker leather covered in dirt and blood.

"Holy shit." Sara quickly limped out from behind the counter. "Guys, call nine-one-one. Marrec!" she yelled toward the back. "Come quick!"

"No. No. I'm fine." The girl waved Sara away.

"Really? You look like shit," Miki observed.

"Bike crashed." The girl stretched and Sara heard every one of the bones cracking. "Actually, that's why I'm here. You've got a mechanic, right?"

Angelina looked the woman over. "Don't you really need an ambulance?"

"Or a hearse," Miki muttered.

Sara elbowed her friend. She did that a lot when it came to Miki.

"Nope. Just a mechanic. And a bathroom."

"I'll show her." Angelina led the girl to the back of the store.

Marrec appeared, oil and dirt smeared on his face, hands and T-shirt. The man was supposedly in his sixties but he seemed more a prematurely graying forty-five. Shorter than Sara but powerfully built, he'd taken Sara under his wing when a self-obsessed junior varsity football player threw her head-first through Marrec's shop door during a fight Miki still claimed wasn't her fault.

"What's going on?" Marrec stood next to Sara, wiping his hands on a rag.

"Some girl got into a crash."

Miki stared out the large glass window. "Christ, look at that girl's bike. She should be dead."

Marrec looked at the bike and his eyes narrowed. "She's walking?"

"Believe it or not," Sara answered. "Angelina took her to the bathroom."

Angelina returned to her two friends. "She's in there now. I'm patiently waiting to hear a thud."

"I'll go check her bike," Marrec mumbled while moving toward the exit.

After about ten minutes, the girl re-emerged. She had cleaned off her face and hands and rinsed the blood and dirt from her hair. A surprisingly pretty girl—who looked like she could bench press a Buick.

"Much better," she announced. She focused on the three women who stared back. "Something wrong?"

"We're just waiting for you to pass out," Miki admitted.

The girl grinned. "Mechanic?"

"That's Marrec. He's checking your bike now." Sara glanced out the window. "But, honey, your bike is toast."

"Ya think?" She walked outside, Sara Miki and Angie following behind her.

Sara marveled at how quickly the girl seemed to be recovering. Maybe she was on some new painkiller. Sara would have to ask. She might need it herself soon.

The girl walked over to the mangled remains of her bike. "My poor baby."

Sara caught Miki rolling her eyes. Her short friend never could understand the bikers' love of their choppers. The passion.

Marrec, who still crouched beside the bike, slowly stood and glowered at the girl. Their eyes locked and they stared at each other. That's all they did. Just stared. Finally, the girl turned away.

Miki nudged Sara, but Sara blew it off. She'd seen Marrec do that many times before. It was that "weird thing" he did. Sometimes even to his own sons or wife. Hell, Miki did lots of weird things so she had absolutely no room to judge.

"Where did you crash anyway?" Angelina asked.

The girl knelt down beside the mangled metal. "Don't know. I guess about two miles back."

The friends exchanged glances.

"How did you get your bike here?"

"Dragged it." The girl's head tilted to the side as Marrec turned to face the parking lot entrance.

"Wait a minute." Miki didn't even bother trying to hide her disbelief. "You expect us to believe you dragged that thing here? In your condition? Bullshit," she finished flatly.

As always, Miki was as subtle as a brick to the head.

The girl ignored her and said, "Good." She seemed relieved. "They're here." She stood and walked to the front of the parking lot as four beautiful, tricked-out choppers, all manned by women, pulled in and halted next to the girl.

"Check it out." Angelina elbowed her friends. "Lesbians. In Texas."

"Would you shut up." Sara chuckled.

"Julie, glad to see you're not dead," spoke the oldest of the women. Her blonde hair was streaked with gray, her face covered in age lines. She was probably gorgeous once. Now merely beautiful.

Sliding off her bike, the older woman hugged the battered girl. "You sure you're okay?"

"Yeah, Casey. I'm fine." The girl leaned in and whispered something. Casey looked up and straight at Marrec.

"No problem." Casey walked over to Marrec. "This your shop?"

Sara watched her boss's back straighten, his arms crossing over his large chest. "Yeah."

The woman smiled coldly. "Got a minute?"

Marrec observed the woman carefully. "Sara," he spoke without taking his eyes off Casey. "Go inside."

A startled Sara glanced at her equally startled friends. "Are you kidding?" He *must* be kidding. Marrec rarely ordered her to do anything. He especially never ordered her to go away like a ten-year-old child.

The expression he gave her clearly told her he was serious. But before Sara could clearly and concisely tell him to fuck off, Casey intervened.

"Julie needs to get a new bike. That one isn't going anywhere. Could you show her what you guys have?"

Sara snorted at the lame attempt to get rid of her.

"Wow, Julie. Your ride is fucked." That low-voiced statement from a tiny Asian woman crouching by the totaled bike.

"I know, Kelly. I know."

"Don't worry about it," Casey offered. "We'll get you a new one here. Kelly's got the cash and cards. I think it's time to spend a little money."

Miki folded her arms in front of her chest. "Drug money, I assume," she queried smugly.

Angelina's eyes snapped open wide and Sara slapped her hand over her friend's mouth. Casey raised one eyebrow, looking right at Sara. Like she could control Miki or something. Hell, no one could control Miki.

"Why don't you guys go in and check out our stock," Sara quickly stated. "Some great stuff just came in."

With a nod, Casey motioned to her females and they entered the store while she and Marrec walked to the edge of the parking lot, out of hearing range. Once they were effectively alone, Sara and Angelina let out huge sighs.

"Drug money, I assume?" Angelina ground out between clenched teeth, giving Miki a good shove.

Miki shrugged. "I was just asking."

"Well don't. Don't ask. Don't query. Don't question." Angelina moved toward the door, then spun around on four-inch designer heels to glare at Miki. "And try *not* to get the shit kicked out of us by biker chicks. Think you can handle that?"

"Think you can handle that," Miki angrily mimicked as she went to follow Angelina into the store. Sara watched as Miki grabbed the handle on the glass door, but she pushed instead of pulled and slammed into it. "Motherfucker!"

Sara laughed and felt her headache slip away.

Chapter Two

"So, what happened to your face?"

Sara grabbed Miki by the back of her T-shirt and jeans before the woman could dive over the counter and wrap her hands around the throat of the Asian girl they called Kelly.

She pulled Miki back to her while Angelina leaned forward and said, "You know what they say about curiosity? That it stabbed the annoying biker girl over and over and over again until she spit up blood."

Oh, yeah. That was subtle. Sara pushed Angelina back, too. Her friends had always been protective of her. It was sweet, in its own rabid-squirrel kind of way.

People rarely just came out and asked about her wounds. Not so directly. Yet there seemed to be no malice to Kelly's question. It was simply a question. So, Sara gave her a very simple answer. "None of your business. So are you taking those shirts?"

Kelly looked down at the six T-shirts she held in her hand. "Uh…yeah. Sure."

As Sara rung up the sale, Marrec and Casey returned. The tension seemed to have lessened, but she could tell Marrec was still on edge as he walked around the counter, patting Sara on the shoulder. "Everything okay?"

"Yeah," Sara said under her breath. "And they're buying a ton of shit. I expect a bonus, old man."

Marrec smiled. "Greedy bitch."

Casey stood in front of Sara, examining her closely. "Interesting scar."

"Un-fucking-believable," Miki bit out, looking like she might try and dive over the counter again.

"Check this out." Casey pulled her mane of hair off her neck, and turned so Sara had a clear view.

Angelina and Miki winced.

The healed over and raised rips across the woman's neck ran from the back of her left ear, across and down her neck, disappearing under her jacket. Sara sensed they went on well down her torso.

"Mountain lion," Casey volunteered. "Eight years ago. A nasty fight."

"You? You fought a mountain lion?" Clearly Miki wasn't buying it.

"It was either him or me. And in the end it all comes down to survival."

Sara thought about her father. He'd fought to protect her all those years ago and it cost him his life, but in the end she survived.

Julie, who seemed to be getting stronger and healthier by the minute, interrupted the moment with an announcement. "The males are here."

Four more bikes pulled up outside the shop. Sara could see the gorgeous chrome through the window. She got all tingly just thinking about having one of those bikes between her legs.

Miki turned to Casey. "Are these men *men* or chicks dressed as men?" Sara sighed and Angelina closed her eyes in exasperation. Miki grinned. "I'm just askin'."

What walked through the shop door three minutes later, though, were clearly "men *men*."

Chapter Three

"You know," Angelina quietly stated to her two friends, "I was just thinking I need to stop by the butcher. Pick up some steak."

"I could use some sausage," Sara added. Then she and Angelina began giggling over the "hottie-hots" who walked into Marrec's store.

"Aren't you two freaked out by these people just a little bit?" Miki demanded softly.

Sara watched the group interaction. She had to admit, they didn't act like any motorcycle club she'd ever met before. Friendly but polite. Affectionate and playful, but not remotely sexual, except for a few.

A tall, amazing-looking man walked over to Casey. His hair was grayer than the woman's, but it looked premature. There were only a few lines on his face. As soon as Casey saw him she broke into a huge smile. A smile he returned. He didn't kiss her hello. Instead, he brushed his head gently against hers. Nuzzled her under the chin, pulled her hair aside and licked the wound on the back of her neck.

Angie missed the moment, busy staring at her hands and complaining about her chipped nail polish. But Miki saw it.

"Okay. Does *that* freak you out?"

Sara shrugged and answered honestly, "I think it was kinda sweet. Weird, but sweet." She was used to bikers grabbing their women's crotches and shoving their tongues down their throats right in the middle of the shop. It always seemed like they were about to take them right there on the show floor. But what she'd just witnessed, that was affection. Something she herself had never really experienced with the men she had gone out with over the years. Nice men she'd only let get so close. There was never a time she didn't have walls up or, as her friends called it, "The Armor". She felt safer that way, but it also kept every well-meaning man at arm's length.

Another male came in. This one blond and perhaps a little closer to her age. He was as big as a house, though. Like a blond polar bear. All muscle and strength. He actually reminded Sara of the Vikings from one of Miki's computer games. All he needed was that horned helmet. He greeted a few of the females but mostly with a pat on the shoulder or a nod. But when he saw Miki it was like someone hit him over the head with a rock. He looked stunned. He walked into the wall.

Sara turned to Marrec in an attempt to hide her smile. He'd gone over to greet the older biker as Casey spoke quietly to him. When she was done, the two men stared at each other and, finally, shook hands. "Name's Yates. And I really appreciate this," he said with genuine warmth.

Marrec nodded. "No problem. Just remember whose territory this is."

Yates smiled at that. "I don't think that's a problem."

Sara and Miki frowned at each other. Sara had never known Marrec to be so territorial before. Bikers came in to his shop all the time, but he never seemed concerned about any of them as he did this group. And these people seemed positively kittenish compared to some of the hardcore criminals who'd walked through the doors of Marrec's business over the years.

Of course, all this had Miki's major brainpower working on hyperdrive. And Sara knew her friend was on the verge of saying something completely inappropriate—again.

Angelina, however, was busy putting on lip gloss while staring into a mirror customers used to try on sunglasses. Angie was one woman who didn't let herself get worked up over stuff she couldn't control. Although that rather Zen-like philosophy did take years of court-ordered therapy to obtain.

"Oh, God. Oh, God," Miki whispered desperately. Sara watched the blond bear meandering toward them with the possible intent of trying to talk to Miki. Turning to Sara with a look of pure panic, Miki yelped, "Tell me he's not coming over here."

"Not everyone is loved by Thor, God of Thunder."

Miki glared but couldn't stifle a laugh. "I hate you."

Sara grinned, about ready to help her friend escape true love—but *he* walked in.

He'd been outside checking out the damaged bike. He was tall. Taller than Yates. Taller than any of them, except for the big blond guy who kept silently staring at Miki and slowly moving in on her. This new guy was big too. Sara actually wondered how he possibly got those shoulders through the door. And at six-feet, there were not a lot of men who made her feel small.

Dark brown hair reached to his shoulders and swept across his face, practically covering bright hazel-colored eyes. He had several days' growth of stubble on his jaw, and a thick muscular neck she could spend all day chewing and licking. Dressed in black jeans, black T-shirt and a black leather jacket, he was, simply, the most beautiful man Sara had ever seen in her life. And she wanted him so badly she couldn't breathe.

He didn't notice her when he walked in, but everyone else did. The rest of the members stopped talking, stopped shopping, stopped moving. As one, they all lifted their heads and sniffed the air. Then they all turned and looked at Sara.

She couldn't understand it. She hadn't done anything. Hadn't moved. She'd also stared at Yates when he walked in. Exactly what cued them in to her sudden need to be naked and straddling this brown-haired god, she had no idea.

As she obsessed over this, Angelina leaned in and said, "Um…hon? Are we going to need to peel you off that seat?"

Sara, distracted from being the center of attention, turned to Angelina. "Shut up."

"You don't remember him," Miki chastised, her blond stalker quickly forgotten.

"Remember who?

"Tragic, black leather–clad biker guy over there."

Angie started laughing. "Oh, my God, it *is* him."

"Who?" Sara snapped.

Before she got an answer, Sara realized that after greeting the females of the group, he'd finally noticed her. His eyes locked on her and she actually felt her face get hot and the walls of her pussy tighten.

"The good Samaritan," Miki offered.

"I think your exact words were," Angelina added in, "'Pretty man is all mine'."

"Just before you stuck your tongue down his throat," Miki filled in.

"And I believe there was some crotch-grabbing." Angelina shook her head. "Whore."

Sara growled at her friends when the insanity from the previous evening came flooding back to her. Too much tequila. Asshole club pigs grabbing her. And the classic Sara-drinking stupidity, where she did something she ended up regretting the following morning. Apparently, this time her regret was him.

"Oh, hell."

"But clearly he remembers *you*." Angelina giggled.

Of course he did. When a tall, scarred woman calls you a pretty man, and sticks her tongue down your throat—you remembered her. And if Sara had any doubt, the sudden grin on his face confirmed it.

"Uh-oh," Angelina whispered.

"He's headin' this way," Miki chimed in. Fuck, she almost sang it.

"I'm in hell." Sara began to search for something, *anything* to do. She was too distracted to focus, though. Her nipples had hardened. Her pussy was on fire. And she kept wondering what he looked like completely naked.

Naked with his head between her thighs.

Jesus Christ! What was wrong with her?

"Hi." His voice was so deep she felt like he'd run a finger up her bare back. He leaned against the counter and lowered his head so they were eye to eye.

"Howdy!" Angelina piped up, a big smile on her beautiful face.

"Hey, y'all!" Miki said, her Texan accent suddenly ten times thicker than normal.

Sara hated them both. A lot.

Still she wasn't going to let some guy freak her out. Sara looked up, a greeting on her lips, but it caught in her throat.

He was staring at her—well, more like smirking—with those beautiful eyes of his, and really it was all she could do to stop herself from giving him a hickey on that thick neck.

"Remember me? I'm your...what was it? Oh, yeah. I'm your pretty man. But I never quite got your name."

Sara could *feel* her face getting red when the entire room erupted into laughter.

Before she could say a word—or punch him in the face—Yates interrupted. "All right people, let's saddle up. Julie, we'll pick up your new bike tomorrow."

Marrec came back behind the counter and Angelina moved out of the way so he could get to the safe her long legs were in front of.

"You three." Casey stood next to Sara's deepest, darkest fantasy and Sara didn't like it one damn bit. In fact, she wanted to punch the shit out of the bitch for standing way too close to him, which was clearly not a rational response when she didn't even know the guy. "Because you were so helpful today," Casey continued, oblivious to how close she was to getting her throat ripped out, "I'd like to invite you to a little party we're throwing out near that big park off the state highway."

"Kingsley Park?" Angelina practically knocked a crouching Marrec over to get closer to Casey. The woman did love a good party.

"Yeah, that's it," Casey confirmed. "I think you guys will have a good time."

"Or," Miki interjected flatly, "you could cut our throats and leave us for dead now so we don't have to make the trip."

Sara knew she no longer had anyone's attention. Miki and her mouth had thankfully stolen the spotlight once again.

Everyone stared at Miki—except *her* pretty man. He was still staring at Sara, but he did raise an eyebrow at Miki's comment.

Marrec quickly stood. "Miki!"

"What?" she asked with that damned innocent smile.

Marrec took a deep breath, something the older man often did around Miki. "You guys, go to the party. Have a great time. I will personally vouch for these people."

Angelina answered for the three of them, "We'll be there."

"Great. Ten p.m., day after tomorrow. See you then." With that, Casey walked out of the store, the females following her, all loaded down with bags of Harley-and Marrec's Choppers–branded clothes.

"Let's go, gentlemen. We've got beer to buy." The men moved out, but Yates waited. "Zach, let's hit it."

Zach stared at Sara for a few more moments, straightened up and followed Yates to the door. "Tequila, right?" Sara watched him as he moved, she couldn't help herself—the man had an amazing ass. "That's your drink of choice?"

Then he was gone.

"Sara's got a hottie on her tail." Angelina practically frothed at the mouth in her excitement.

"More like a biker. And they're on the List," Miki pointed out.

"Fuck the List! She needs to get laid," Angelina barked back.

Miki sighed. "Not if her last fuck will be a train pulled by some scumbag motorcycle club."

"Okay!" Sara grabbed each by the shoulder. "Marrec here is as close as I've had to a father since I was eight. I would really appreciate the two of you not discussing me and fucking in the man's presence. Do you think you idiots could handle that?"

Miki and Angelina were silent for a moment. But it was just a moment.

"Did you see the bulge in the man's pants? He's packing major heat and it's for her."

"*He's on the List!*"

She was much prettier than he remembered. And sweeter. She actually blushed when he looked at her. She wasn't remotely innocent, though. He smelled her lust from fifty feet away—as did everyone else. What surprised him even more was his body's immediate response to it. To her. Which seemed strange. The woman wasn't anything to him.

"Cute, huh, Zach?" Casey sat on the bike behind Yates. Her arm around her mate's torso, her head on his shoulder.

"You're leaving your bike here?"

"Marrec will take care of it. So, what do you think?"

"I think that with all due respect, you should back the fuck off."

Casey grinned. "Don't take it out on me because you're afraid to make a move."

"Afraid to make a move? Really?" Zach shook his head. "I wish I could figure out what you're up to." He turned and looked at Yates' mate. The Alpha Female of his pack. Affectionately known by him and his baby sister as the bitch from hell. "You've never given a shit about what I stick my dick in to before, why do you suddenly care now?"

"I don't. I only care about the Pack. And, unfortunately, that includes you." She flashed him a grin as Yates started his bike.

"So what exactly are you hoping I'll do?"

Casey shrugged. "Follow your instincts."

Zach Sheridan watched them pull out, annoyed his mother raised him not to hit women in the face.

He walked to his bike and stopped. He looked back through the store windows. She used her arms to haul herself onto the counter. What strength she lacked in her bad leg, she made up for in the rest of her body. Lifting her legs, she twisted her butt around, and slid down off the case so she was in front of the counter. Her friends appeared to be arguing. She stood between them, trying to stop the fight, but the two women were in full swing. Finger pointing had begun.

Zach straddled his bike, but he couldn't resist looking back one more time. It seemed she'd gotten tired of the fight. She grabbed both her friends by the face and shoved them in opposite directions. Zach laughed, causing Conall, who had been waiting for him, to stare.

"Did you just laugh or am I delusional?"

Only Conall could get away with making fun of his less-than-impressive sense of humor. Anyone else, Zach would have kicked them in the teeth.

"Those women are crazy," he offered as explanation.

"Yeah," Conall agreed. "But so cute."

Zach turned to his big, blond friend. He'd grown up with Conall and knew exactly what he liked. "The little black one, right?"

"Zacharias, I don't notice color."

"Maybe not. But you noticed the tight ass in those jeans."

"Yes. That I did notice."

"Did you also happen to notice the mouth that ass was attached to?"

"There's nothing wrong with having an opinion."

"If that logic helps you get through the night."

"*She'd* help me get through the night."

"Shame she didn't even notice you were in the room."

"Unlike yours. Jesus, I thought she was going to mount you right there."

Chapter Four

Zach and Conall arrived at their temporary den a few minutes after everyone else. The women had done a good job of finding a place with solid hunting, a lake nearby, and thick woods that allowed for privacy. Julie and Kelly were already on their cell phones making arrangements. They had the best connections and could have the place set and ready in no time.

Zach was about to head down to the lake and maybe get in some hunting but Yates called him and a few of the others over.

"Well?" He wanted their opinion on the female.

"She's fucking clueless," Jake, a recent addition to the Pack, offered. "How's that possible?"

"We can thank that bitch Lynette. She raised her. So just telling her the truth ain't an option. She'll never believe it."

"But," Conall added, "they're already here. I smelled them on the outskirts of town."

"So, the question remains. Do we just take her?" Yates looked at Zach. He'd been doing that a lot lately, seeking his council.

Zach shook his head. "I wouldn't. She's squirrely. We take her now, she might snap on us. And the aggression's already there. She's about three tequilas away from losing it completely."

"Sure we shouldn't just put her down?" Jake asked. "She is seriously wounded."

Zach turned to look at him. He knew Jake was young, but he was starting to discover Jake was stupid too. Still, the young wolf looked away—he wouldn't try and stare Zach down. He knew better. He still had scars on the back of his neck from Zach quietly explaining his place in the Pack.

"That's not an option," Zach stated calmly.

"Fine." Yates nodded. "We watch her and we wait. But remember, we're on Marrec's territory. Be nice." He looked directly at Zach.

"What are you lookin' at me for? I'm a ray of fuckin' sunshine."

"You're an asshole."

Zach shrugged. "It's a flaw."

"I'm glad you're so comfortable with the real you." Yates smiled. "You take first watch tonight with Conall."

"Babysitting?" Zach didn't bother trying to hide his annoyance. He hated babysitting and hated the thought of sitting around watching that adorable piece of ass from the woods.

Yates snorted and walked off, tossing back over his shoulder, "Every princess needs her knight."

Zach sighed. "Princess my ass."

ଓ ଓ ଓ

Four hours since they left Marrec's shop. Four hours and these two crazy bitches were *still* arguing, but now they'd moved on to clothes. What Sara shouldn't wear and what she should wear. Miki pushed for something conservative and easy to run in should they have to "Make a break for it." Angelina wanted Sara in something classy but hot that would have Zach "Fucking her on his bike." Sara had no intention of wearing any of their suggestions. But her two friends were like rabid dogs. Once they started arguing it was hard to get them to stop. Sara tried to escape when she closed up the store for Marrec, but they'd argued all the way over to her beat-up white pickup and got in with her. Such a shame she stopped keeping her shotgun in her gun rack.

Sara sighed and shifted on her bed, trying to ease the pain in her right leg. Honestly, the things she put up with. They were extremely lucky she loved them both so much. Otherwise, she might have killed them by now.

And while they argued and threatened, Sara obsessed and worried. Her leg had gotten worse the past couple of months and she didn't know why. It never fully healed after she and her father were attacked, although to the naked eye it simply looked like a badly healed wound. That's why she'd been drinking the other night. It was the only thing that truly dulled the pain and her brain. It had become a constant challenge for her to battle the voices in her head that told her nothing was right. Her body wasn't right. She wasn't right. Her life was a mess. A boring mess, but a mess. Sara didn't exactly live on the wild side. That night of drinking was about as wild as she got, and the only thing she remembered doing was kissing a stranger. A really gorgeous stranger. He had the thickest neck, and those beautiful hazel eyes just seemed to...

Sara shifted again. This time not from the pain in her legs but the throbbing between them.

This was ridiculous. She was a nice girl. Not a whore. Men either treated her with the utmost respect or they were cruel about her scars. There was no in-between. They either treated her like a princess or treated her like a freak. Not Zach, though. No, he treated her like she was hot. But she wasn't the "hot friend". She was the sensible friend. Angelina was the hot friend. The reason guys became friends with Sara in the first place. Angelina wore designer clothes and expensive high-heeled shoes. She was the only woman Sara knew who would come to Skelly's on Goth night wearing a champagne-colored dress—her "signature color" as Angelina called it—matching heels, and a purse.

Miki was the brilliant, super-cute friend. She was the one who could diffuse the bomb in thirty seconds with bubble gum, toothpaste and a binder clip while still looking cute in a belly shirt. Miki was working on her third master's degree because she thought the whole "PhD thing" was so overplayed. Miki was the one in high school who hadn't been able to use a computer or phone for three years "as per court order" and knew all the M.O.s of serial killers from the Twentieth Century because every woman should know the warning signs of a serial killer. "What if you're dating one?" she'd always ask with a smile, before giving a gruesome detail or two about some murderer.

And then there was Sara. Reliable, dependable Sara. "The Golden Retriever of the group," her grandmother once sneered at her over dinner. She was always the "good buddy" or the "little sister". She was never the "piece of ass". And after twenty-eight years she'd learned to accept that fate. She accepted it like the pain in her leg and the scar on her face. It was there and it was who she was. Might as well just deal with it.

Until *he* came along. Zach. She thought she'd dreamed that kiss. That amazing freakin' kiss. Part of her wished she had. The reality of it getting a little too much to bear. A little too stressful. Shit, she'd been drunk. Drunk-Sara was fun. Drunk-Sara set things on fire. Drunk-Sara grabbed groping men by the balls and squeezed until they passed out. There was no way Golden Retriever Sara could compete with Drunk-Sara. And Drunk-Sara was a liability.

Sara didn't remember much about the night besides the kiss and someone grabbing her while she was on the way to the bathroom. And beautiful man saved her. She still remembered the feel of his lips against hers and the impressive bulge in her hand when she'd massaged his cock. And, for some unknown reason, she was obsessed with his teeth. She just couldn't remember why.

Sara sighed. She could still hear her friends yelling. Something about a thong and how she wasn't a slut...unlike some people.

Sara scooted off the bed and stormed into the living room. No use yelling at them, then it would be three crazy women yelling. Instead, she went to her stereo system and turned on some loud techno music from a DJ in Germany.

Miki and Angelina continued to yell for another minute, until they realized they couldn't hear themselves much less each other. They turned to stare at Sara. When she was certain she had their full attention, she turned the music down, but not off.

"Are you two done?"

"She started it," Angelina complained.

"*I* started it?" Miki snapped.

"That's it!" Sara yelled. She walked to her kitchen and grabbed three beers from the refrigerator. "Here." She handed one each to her friends. "You two bitches are making me nuts." Sara opened the ice cold can and took a swig. "Besides, it doesn't matter what I wear." She took another swallow of beer. "I don't have a chance in hell with a guy like that."

Sara went to her front door, determined to sit on her porch and enjoy the cool night. But Miki's cutting voice caused her to trip on the doorframe and stumble outside. "If we'd left the store, he would have fucked you on the counter."

Concealed behind trees, Zach watched Sara's place. "I want you at her house," Yates had ordered after he'd argued. "Make sure she doesn't have any more surprise visits."

Yeah, he hated babysitting duty and Yates knew it. But Zach put up with it...for now. Because everyone understood, clearly even Yates, that Zach would be making a move to be Pack leader. He was ready. And Zach wanted it. He was just waiting for the right time to move. He loved Yates like a brother, but the man was getting weak. It wasn't age either. It was his woman. Casey was tough but toxic. Far too human for the role. Wanting power. Her primary concern, no matter what she said, was not the Pack, but her standing within it. The females put up with her, but he could tell that wouldn't last much longer. His sister, who had been traveling for about a year, had a good shot at becoming Alpha Female, but he wasn't sure she even wanted it or would leave Europe to come get it.

That's why Casey's recent foray into the past was an obvious tactic to keep Zach busy and out of the way. She never cared about Bruce Morrighan's missing offspring before. In fact, they all knew Sara'd been taken by her grandmother after the brutal killing of the girl's father. And although Casey thought she could keep Zach away for weeks "monitoring the girl", as she put it, they never expected the Pride to actually be hunting the woman. Finish off the job they'd started so long ago. But Pride females were notoriously patient. They'd probably known where Morrighan's offspring was for years, but no one, absolutely *no one,* would even think about going up against Lynette Redwolf.

Why? Because the bitch was crazy.

A Native American and a shapeshifter, Lynette rejected both aspects early on. Instead she tried to become a "normal woman". She buried the

Beast and stayed human. The fact that she'd come from a long line of shapeshifting shamans apparently meant nothing to her.

Her plan had been to raise her daughter, Kylie, the same. But Kylie figured out what she was by the time she was fourteen. At eighteen, she met her mate and Sara's father, Bruce Morrighan. His family dated back to the sixteenth century. A tough Scottish clan of wolves that had done serious damage to the land before they'd gained control over their need to kill. Like Zach, Bruce was born and raised as part of the Magnus Pack. It was the only world he'd ever known. Until he met Kylie. Their mating supposedly one for the record books, their passion scorching the Colorado Mountains where they found each other. Bruce on a camping trip. Kylie trying to escape her controlling mother by working as a waitress in a local diner. Once they were marked and mated, the couple seemed to become more wolf than human. Staying in wolf form for days on end, they slept, hunted and lived the majority of their lives as wolves. When Sara was born, the Pack felt certain she would certainly become Alpha Female one day.

But then Kylie fucked with Annie Withell, head of the Withell Pride, and all hell broke loose.

During a confrontation, Kylie somehow killed the four-hundred-pound Annie and started a Pack-Pride war that continued to this day. By the time Sara was one-year-old, Kylie's torn and half-eaten wolf carcass had been dumped at the front door of the Pack's den.

Bruce had been inconsolable. With the help of several Pack mates and against the Alpha leader's orders, he attacked the Pride, killing two of its prime breeding males. Then Bruce took his daughter and left. Moved to Arizona. And everything went quiet, until the pair went on a hunting trip in an Arizona state park. No one knew the details, but Bruce's human remains were found beside the campsite.

Sara was missing for a day, but eventually located twenty miles from where they found her father's body. Unconscious next to a riverbank, her face torn like it had hit jagged rock. Her leg ripped as if hit by an animal paw. She was in a coma for a week and no one thought she would survive. Then Lynette brought her granddaughter here. To this town and these people. A town run by wolves. Marrec was a shapeshifter and so was half the town. He protected and loved Sara like his own daughter. He could have turned her himself but he hadn't.

Yet Marrec's loyalty to Sara was strong. Palpable, in fact. Apparently Casey had to do some fast talking to keep the guy from pushing them off his territory. Maybe now the old bitch was dead, Marrec decided it was time for Sara to know the truth. To know who and what she was. Perhaps he'd waited until he felt the death of her grandmother was far enough away, Sara could more easily learn to accept what she was. But before he had the chance, they'd shown up. The Magnus Pack. Her true father's Pack. Maybe to Marrec having her turned by her father's Pack seemed only fitting. So, in the end, he'd allowed them all to stay without much trouble.

Now here Zach sat with only Conall to keep him company, watching a house on a chilly Texas night. He could see into her home through a window, but all he saw were the two other females still arguing. Boy, could those broads go and go and go.

Sara had disappeared and he was really starting to miss seeing her. Although Conall seemed to be enjoying his view of Miki. The angrier the pint-sized woman got the more Zach could smell Conall's desire for her. *Twisted.* Conall quietly padded by, his white-blond fur ruffled by the light wind coming from the East.

Zach scratched his muzzle with one paw as German techno music hit his ears. *Good* German techno music. In the boonies of Texas? He looked back at the house. The music died after a few moments and a couple of minutes later Sara stumbled onto the porch. She wore baggy sweats and a big hockey shirt. He heard her friends laughing, but he refused to believe they were laughing at the fact she seemed to have trouble walking. He'd hate to have to kick their asses.

Sara was laughing, though, and he realized he was getting protective over a woman he didn't know and really didn't want to know. He had no plans of getting all tangled up with a female. Especially not this female.

A good one-hundred feet from the house, Zach could still hear her clearly. "I hate both of you!" she yelled as her friends came out on to the porch. Sara straddled the banister and, boy, did he envy that banister, while Miki hit the swing and Angelina sat on the stairs.

He marveled at how they went from full-on screaming one minute to hysterical laughter the next.

And he wished he could have heard what they had been talking about in the house because Sara's next sentence completely intrigued him…

"But forget about me. I think Miki's the one with the chance to get laid."

"Don't start," Miki warned.

"He was like the dog," Angelina offered, "and you were like the chew toy on top of the cabinet. He couldn't quite reach it but he wouldn't stop staring at it." Sara burst into another round of laughter while Miki looked like she was about to lob her beer at Angelina but changed her mind and took a long swig instead.

"But," Angelina continued, "no one seemed the least bit interested in me."

"Well, of course not," Sara answered. "You have no obvious physical flaws and you weren't balls-out rude. Why would they be interested in you?"

The three women laughed some more at that. Then they drank their beer and quietly listened to the night.

Zach couldn't take his eyes off Sara. She was so beautiful. And when she leaned back and stretched, a low growl coming from her throat that he felt more than heard, it took all his control not to charge over there and drag her beautiful ass back into the house and to her bed.

"We should go hunting next week," Angelina offered. "Work off some of that aggression."

"Yeah, Miki."

"She's talking to you, bonehead."

Sara was floored. "What are you guys talking about?"

"Oh, come on. When you told that biker last week you were going to shove your fist up his ass?"

"He touched my tits."

"You've got big tits," Miki muttered.

"And when you threw that helmet at Marrec?"

"I missed."

"Barely," Miki added.

"Would you shut up," Sara snapped at Miki. Both her friends smirked at her, and Sara realized they were right. She had been aggressive lately. Really aggressive. Perhaps dangerously so. But she didn't know why.

She took a deep breath. "Sorry. I'm sorry. I'm just stressed."

"Your leg?" Angelina gently asked.

"It's nothing serious," Sara lied. "It'll be fine." She smiled at her friends. "Really."

Angelina and Miki exchanged glances, but moved on.

"So," Angelina said, "that Zach's quite a piece of ass, huh?"

"We are so not having that conversation." The three friends laughed as Sara felt her face get red with embarrassment. "Bitches."

Zach gave Conall a wolfish grin. He had to admit, it was nice being referred to as a "piece of ass".

He watched Sara lie to her friends. And she was lying. The girl was in a momentous amount of pain, but she hid it amazingly well. She was a lot stronger than any of the Pack, himself included, gave her credit for.

Sara finished her beer, crinkling the can with one strong hand. "I'm thinking about getting a new dog." Well that came out of nowhere. And based on her friends' reactions they were none too pleased.

"Oh, for fuck sake," Miki snapped.

"I thought you guys liked dogs."

"I'm a cat person," Angelina volunteered. Zach had already guessed that.

"I like dogs. Not the dogs you get, though. You always pick some scraggly-ass stray off the street and try to make it a pet."

"You could get a cat," Angelina offered hopefully.

"Agents of Satan? No thank you. I like my eyes right where they are. In my head."

"Ladies." Angelina sighed. "Is this what we're reduced to? Are we going to be…" she wore an expression of utter disgust, "…pet people?"

"I can't." Miki leaned her head to the side to stretch the muscles, and Zach heard Conall give a low growl. "No pets. No plants."

Sara smirked. "You mean anything needing actual care?"

Miki gave a dismissive wave of her hand. "It's just too much to remember."

"Please tell me you're not going to breed."

"It's just," Angelina began to whine and Sara knew what was coming, "I don't want us to end up three old maids, living in a house with several hundred cats."

"That won't happen." Miki happily stretched her whole body. She did love to forecast. "I'll be kidnapped by Black Ops. They'll be hoping to use my brilliance against this government's enemies."

Sara and Angelina looked at each other.

"Your brilliance?" Sara asked.

Miki ignored her, like she always did during this conversation. "Angelina will marry someone very wealthy but cold. She'll last about ten years, then she'll plot, plan and execute his murder. Get away with it. And marry a younger man. Maybe even his first-born, teenaged son."

"Hey!" Angelina never liked that future prediction.

"And Sara…" Miki looked at her friend. "She doesn't like cats."

"I don't like cats? That's the best you can do? How about 'And Sara will live happily ever after with Mr. Doesn't-get-on-her-nerves-too-much.' Why can't I have that?"

"You're too picky."

"It's not my fault that scarred, damaged women aren't high on the market. And I'm not going to take any old thing thrown at me."

"You're too picky," Angelina confirmed. "Because I remember a few interested individuals who weren't too bad. Trevor."

"Too strict," Miki explained.

"Fred."

"Too neat."

"Bobby Joe."

"Too tall."

"Mike."

"Too short."

"Okay. Okay. I get it." Sara didn't need to hear this. All those bad attempts at relationships had happened years ago. The well had been quite dry for some time.

"Wait. There's still my personal favorite. Kenny Ray."

"Too nice."

"Nice?" Sara scoffed. "He said I was boring. How is that nice?"

Angelina gave a wicked smile. "Too nice in bed."

"Oh. Yeah. He was." Sara shuddered. "Yuck." She remembered actually throwing him out of bed. Out of bed and across the room. Odd. Maybe she was drinking that night too.

"I bet Zach's not nice." Angelina's smile became more wicked, if that were possible. "I bet he's not nice at all. In bed or out."

"He's on the List," Miki reminded them.

"But he doesn't look like a biker, does he? You know, he actually looks like he bathes. Besides, I'm not talking marriage. I'm talking about getting control of your aggression."

Sara looked at her friend of twenty years. "Dear God, woman. Are you talking about him *fucking* the aggression out of me?"

The women began laughing hysterically.

"I'm not seeing the problem here, people," Angelina explained. "You get in. Do what you have to do and get out."

"That's it!" Sara laughingly yelled. "We're not having this discussion anymore."

"You should just think about it. That's all I'm saying."

"No. I'm a nice girl. I'm not a whore." Her friends didn't say a word. "I'm not."

Angelina shrugged. "You keep believing that."

Sara tossed her crushed beer can, barely missing her friend's head.

Angelina didn't even turn around. Instead she looked out into the darkness. "It's such a beautiful night."

Sara grinned. "Yup." Her grin widened. "And it's about that time."

Miki closed her eyes. "I hate this."

Sara leaned back. "Sssh. Listen."

A moment later, Zach heard the first howl. Full-bloods. He'd smelled them as soon as he stepped onto her property. He'd been waiting for hours for them to give him a hard time about being in their territory and for not being full wolf—they were amazingly snobby about that sort of thing. But, to his surprise, they still hadn't bothered him or Conall. Maybe the full-bloods knew they were there to protect Sara.

Because when they howled, their howls were for Sara and Sara alone.

Miki cringed. Angelina looked unimpressed still rocking to the German techno coming from the house. But Sara's eyes were closed and she was smiling. Then, she howled back.

"Sara," Miki warned with a laugh. "I swear to God, those things come over here, I'm leaving your ass right on this damn porch."

Sara's smile didn't change. "Pussy," she muttered. She howled again. The wolves answered, and all Zach wanted to do was go to her. To heed her call.

Angelina wrinkled up her pretty nose. "Aren't you worried they'll come down here looking for who's howling back?"

Sara shrugged. "I find them on my porch all the time." At that, Miki jumped up and went into the house. "They never give me any trouble, but I always remember they're wild animals. This is more their territory than mine."

Miki stood behind the living-room window. She opened it so she was still part of the conversation, but could easily close it if "they" decided to attack. She had no idea, however, that window couldn't protect her from shit.

"Besides, they've always made me feel safe. And when I had to live here with her, they always made me feel like I wasn't alone."

"Well," Miki advised, "now you've got us." Sara and Angelina turned and looked at her. "See?" Miki held up a cordless phone. "Nine-one-one is a quick dial away."

"That's it. We're done." Angelina stood abruptly and brushed off her rear with a well-manicured hand. "Let's meet tomorrow morning for coffee at the bookstore."

Miki snorted. "So you can get free coffee from me again, you cheap bitch?"

"And the newspaper. And it's *Mistress* Cheap Bitch to you." Angelina motioned to Sara. "Can we take your truck? Not feeling the walk tonight."

"Yeah. Sure." Then to Miki, "The keys are on the—"

"Yeah, I know. I know." Miki disappeared back into the house after closing the window.

Sara slowly lifted her leg and swung it off the banister. "Pick me up tomorrow first."

"You got it." Angelina sauntered down the stairs, heading toward the truck. "Let's go, Mik."

Miki appeared in the door, the truck keys in one hand and a pump-action shotgun in the other. She headed toward the stairs, but Sara grabbed the gun while walking toward her front door. "Not on your life, missy."

"You call to vicious, blood-thirsty animals and then you won't give me anything to defend myself?"

Sara limped into her house. "I've found it's never the animals you have to worry about, Miki. It's the humans."

Miki headed toward the truck as Angelina started it. Over her shoulder she tossed, "I'll remember that when we find your torn, headless carcass."

Interesting girl, Zach decided, and wondered if Conall knew what he was hoping to get himself—and his cock—into.

When the light went off in Sara's house, Zach figured it was time to settle down for the night. But Sara reappeared on the porch, a can of soda in her hand. She limped to the porch swing and just as carefully lowered herself into the contraption. Once sitting, she let out a deep sigh. She drank her soda and rubbed her leg while gazing out at the night.

The wolves called to her again and, with a smile, Sara answered. This time, however, the wolves didn't respond—Zach did. Lifting his muzzle, he released a howl that tore through the night. He called to her. He didn't know why, but it was a desire he couldn't control. A desire he wasn't exactly sure he wanted to control. Zach assumed she would simply respond again as she had for the other wolves, but when he lowered his head, he found her standing. She limped over to the porch rail and leaned against it while she looked out into the forest. She stared right at Zach although he was sure she couldn't see him. She walked to the porch stairs and stood there. Debating whether she should go in search of that howl's owner? Maybe. Zach didn't know. He had no idea what he did would have such an affect on her. To untrained ears, his howl sounded no different from the wolves now heading back to their den. Yet she still knew.

He never found out her intent, though, because she suddenly doubled-over in pain. She gripped her leg and clenched her jaw, holding onto the porch rail until the worst of the pain seemed to pass. When she looked up again, he could see the tears in her eyes from where he stood. She no longer thought about that howl and the howl's owner. He knew, deep in his gut, she only thought about death. Her death. Slowly, like an old woman, she turned and limped back into her house, barely putting any weight on that bad leg.

This time, she didn't come back out until morning.

Chapter Five

Sara slammed on her brakes and Angie pitched forward, her head nearly banging into the dashboard. Her seatbelt the only thing keeping her from doing so.

Staring up at the stoplight—her excuse for hitting her brakes—Sara bit out between gritted teeth, "I'll say it one more time, then I'm gonna beat the shit out of you. Do not mention that man to me again."

"Okay. Okay. Calm yourself."

Angie smoothed back her perfectly coiffed hair and stared out at the nearly empty streets.

If Sara knew Angie would spend the early-morning drive to the coffeehouse going on and on about how hot Zach was and how he looked like he knew how to handle a "big-boned woman", Sara would have never let her back in the truck.

The ride to the shop was only about fifteen minutes from Sara's house, but at the moment it felt like an eternity.

The light turned green and as Sara raised her foot to hit the gas, the truck slowly rolling forward, Angie said, "But I will say that with lips like those, I'm bettin' that man knows how to go down on a woman. And you do love oral sex."

Sara hit the brakes again, pitching Angie forward, then she slapped her friend in the back of her head, knocking out Angie's perfectly coiffed 'do.

"Hey! Do you have any idea how long it took me to get my hair into this chignon?"

Sara went to slap her again but stopped. "Chignon? What the fuck is a chignon? Do you mean that bun you had in the back of your fat head?"

Angie's eyes narrowed and she gave up trying to save her hairstyle, letting her brown hair drop and fall loose around her shoulders. "Heifer."

"Slut."

"Crack whore."

"Hey!"

Startled, the two women looked out the driver's side window at the man standing there. He wasn't local, Sara didn't even recognize him from the nearby town. "Get your scarred ass in gear and move this goddamn truck!"

Sara didn't really have time to register what the man said before she had to grab hold of Angie as her friend reached under the passenger seat for the two-by-four they kept there for "difficult" situations they often found themselves in because of Miki's mouth or Angie's ass.

"Angie, no!"

"Come on, Sara. Let me hurt him. Let me slap him upside that big fat head."

Trying not to laugh, Sara forced Angie back into her seat.

"Calm down. It's okay."

"It's *not* okay, Sara."

"Angie. Calm down. Breathe, dude. Breathe. Just remember five to ten in maximum security. We don't want to have to face that...again...now do we?"

But the look on Angie's face said she'd face it in a heartbeat.

"Is there a problem, Sara?"

Two of Marrec's nephews stood outside the passenger side. She could tell they'd heard everything and they weren't happy. She only had seconds to diffuse this situation. "Naw—" was all she managed before Angie cut her off.

"That asshole called Sara scarred!"

Sara shook her head and sighed. The way they all acted, you'd think she was still ten and prone to crying.

"You guys, it's really not that big a—"

"We'll take care of it. Y'all go on now."

No. No. This wasn't good. "Wait…"

Marrec's nephews stared right at her and that look on their faces said they didn't want an argument. She recognized that expression cause she got it from Marrec so often.

"Okay."

Sara pulled away and she watched in her rear view the two men approach the much smaller man. Yeah, this would get real ugly real fast, but there was nothing she could do about it now.

෴ ෴ ෴

Zach watched Sara's truck stop short again and he started to head over to find out what the hell was wrong with her driving, when that asshole's cruel words rang out over the quiet town. In fact, every shifter on the street locked on the man like Zach had locked on a deer the night before. But before Zach could do anything, two of Marrec's Pack headed over there first and dealt with it.

Christ, what was wrong with him? When did he get all pathetic and protective over some really annoying woman? Never. That's when. And he wouldn't start now.

Conall walked out of the diner and stood behind him. "I'm still hungry."

Shaking his head, Zach watched Sara's truck continue down the street while Marrec's Pack taught a man how to cry. "You just had five plates of waffles. How are you still hungry?"

"I don't see your point."

"Forget it. My life's too short for this discussion."

"How about coffee?"

Zach shrugged. "Whatever. I saw a place up the street."

෬ ෬ ෬

"I don't know, guys." Miki poured cream in her coffee and stared at her friends.

Sara sipped her hot chocolate and stared back. She'd already seen Miki's morning reading material—a book on the world of motorcycle clubs rested on the counter.

Miki's second job was in a local bookstore slash Internet cafe. This meant her little psycho friend had constant access to just enough information to make her dangerous.

"I don't think we should hit that party tonight."

"What?" Angelina snapped, coming out of her coffee-induced haze. When Angelina drank her coffee, she had the ability to completely tune everyone out. Especially Miki.

"We don't know these people, Angie. And I think there's something weird about them."

"You think there's something weird about everyone."

"Yes. And there always is."

Miki sat on a stool by the register, her gaze focusing on Sara. "What do you think?"

"I don't know. I don't feel overly concerned."

Miki shook her head. "It's bugging me."

Sara didn't have time for this. When Miki had one of her "moments", she could analyze something until you begged her to stop. Begged. "Look, Miki, you can come or you can stay home. Your call. But I'm going."

Miki looked at Angelina, causing the woman to raise one delicate eyebrow. "Like you even have to ask."

Miki chuckled. "Fine. I'm going then. I can't let you two out on your own. But no drinking, Sara. I need you to be rational."

"Good luck with that." The mug of hot chocolate was halfway to Sara's lips when his deep but lightly sarcastic voice stopped her. "The rational part that is."

Sara looked up and there he was. Leaning against the door jam, quietly watching her. The morning sun at his broad back, lightening his dark brown hair and setting off his hazel eyes. He once again wore jeans and a black T-shirt emblazoned with a logo for a band she'd never heard of. His big arms crossed in front of his even bigger chest and when he smiled at her he showed gleaming white teeth.

The man simply looked gorgeous without even trying. She hated him.

"What are you doing here?" Sara bit out before she could stop herself.

"That's not very friendly. I thought Texans were friendly."

"Texans are. But I'm not."

Angelina quickly jumped in, "So that party tomorrow, lots of people going to be there?"

Sara stared straight at Zach. He wouldn't turn away, so she didn't either. That went on for about a minute until his large blond friend bringing up the rear, slammed into Zach's back. "Where's the coffee? I'm dyin'."

There was no way those two huge specimens were getting through the door at the same time, so the blond simply forced his way past Zach into the shop, making a direct line for Miki at the counter.

It was Sara's turn to smile as the blond bear forced Zach to move out of the way. But when Zach's eyes once again focused on hers, Sara's breath caught in her throat and her clit started to throb, her nipples became rock hard. She couldn't help it. Those damn eyes tore right through her. Sara turned away before he could see how much he was getting to her and took a sip of her now tepid chocolate. She couldn't even taste it.

The big blond bear stood at the counter staring at Miki.

Miki stared back at him. She reminded Sara of a skittish colt that might bolt at any moment. "Do you actually want something?" Miki asked carefully.

The big guy blinked in confusion, and Sara had the sneaking suspicion he'd been standing there imagining her best friend naked.

"What?" he finally asked.

Miki looked at Sara, panic wafting off her. "Okay, Sara?"

Sara heard the desperation in her friend's voice. *Poor thing.* Sara sighed to herself. Miki simply didn't know how to handle someone who actually liked her.

Of course, Miki would probably say the same about her.

"Want something?" he asked, snapping out of it. "Oh, yeah." He cleared his throat. "Two large coffees to go. Please."

Miki turned away so fast to fill his order she banged into the counter. Sara saw Angelina's body shaking with silent laughter, while Sara dug her fingernails into the palm of her hand to keep from embarrassing poor Miki any more than she'd embarrassed herself.

"So you guys coming to the party tomorrow night?" the blond stalker asked Miki's back as Zach slowly closed the space between him and Sara.

Sara was still turned away from him, but she felt him. Felt him getting closer to her. Felt her body respond. She was terrified he'd touch her, and terrified he wouldn't. And all that "terror" was making her unbelievably wet.

"Wouldn't miss it," Angelina answered, probably because she knew Miki wouldn't. Typical Angelina, she didn't even notice the two gorgeous men right in front of her. Instead, she flipped through one of those fashion magazines Sara found blindingly boring. Some people called Angelina cold. Sara just called her finicky.

Funny thing was, for the first time Sara could remember, neither of these men seemed to notice Angelina. "Thor" couldn't stop staring at Miki. Zach, for some bizarre reason, wouldn't stop staring at her. Even though Sara's back was to him, she felt his eyes on her. Felt them traveling down her body, her chest, her arms, her legs. She kept asking herself why? What could he possibly see in her? Was he a scar freak or a "gimp" fanatic? Maybe he thought he was doing a good deed. Of course, Zach didn't look like the good deed type. Instead he seemed much more like the "I'll make you come so hard your legs will shake but only if I get something out of it" type.

Whatever his type, it was making her crazy and distrustful which, thankfully, was helping her control her desire to take his cock in her mouth.

What is wrong with you?

Angelina tossed the magazine aside and stood. "I've got to get to work." She grabbed her bag and headed toward the door.

"Wait! Don't leave me!" Sara barked loudly before she had a chance to stop herself. They all turned to stare at her. She cleared her throat. "I'm going to be late for work. So I better leave with you."

Angelina cocked her head in confusion. "Since when do you care about being on time—ow!" Sara grabbed Angelina's arm and forced her out of the store.

"*You're both leaving?*" Miki yelled after them, but Sara kept going. She'd have to apologize to Miki later.

Once Sara dragged her friend to the corner, Angelina snatched her arm away. "*What is it with you?*" she demanded, rubbing the red spot Sara caused while desperately clutching her friend.

"Nothing," Sara snapped back.

Angelina gave a dazzling smile. "He's getting to you."

"Who?"

Her friend nodded back to the bookstore. "You know. Mr. Not Nice."

Sara growled in annoyance and turned to make her way up to Marrec's shop.

"Don't worry," Angelina yelled after her. "I won't tell!"

Without turning around, Sara raised her middle finger high in the air and did her best to ignore the laughter that followed.

"She makes great coffee, huh?" Conall asked as he slowly sipped the French-roasted brew. The pair sat on a bench across the street from the bookstore, Zach's body still throbbing from having Sara's hot little ass in his sights. No one had a right to be that cute so early in the morning.

"Yeah. She sure does." Zach took a healthy sip. "But she's still Satan."

Conall smiled. "Then I guess I'll just have to burn."

Zach shook his head. His friend sure did have it bad for a woman who went screaming beyond the realm of blunt. *Well, whatever floats your boat.*

Like Sara. Sara floated Zach's boat. She was such a ripe piece of ass. Okay, she was more than that, and hearing her and her friends talk about him last night like a side of beef wasn't helping. Because Angelina was right. He wasn't nice, in bed or out. And he had the feeling Sara could handle that. Would be in to that. Would be in to him. So he could be inside of her.

But he wasn't about to get caught in that trap. End up like Yates, with some petty, power-hungry bitch as his mate. Why? So he could breed? The Pack hadn't been the same since Casey came along. Not that anyone considered Zach the fun one of the Pack, but he enjoyed everyone else having fun. Now, no one really laughed anymore. Or simply enjoyed themselves, as wolves often liked to do. The situation even forced his sister to move to their European operations so she could get away from what she called "that fun funeral feeling" the den now had. Casey brought a pall over the Magnus Pack Zach would never really be able to forgive the woman for.

He just didn't get it. They were all human enough to fuck and go. He never understood why Yates hadn't. As much as some of them wanted to believe it, they weren't full wolves. They were human, too. They had the power of choice. He decided he wanted to be Alpha Male. He decided he was going to buy this T-shirt. And he didn't go around attacking every bitch in heat. In fact, he went out of his way to stay away from them. He didn't want kids. He'd be more than happy to let the other Pack mates breed and then raise their little whelps to take over when he was too old or tired to hold the leash. But every wolf female he'd met wanted to breed their mate's kid. So, Zach had decided, any mate he chose would be fixed.

But really, in the end, what exactly was the purpose of marking someone as your mate forever? At least full-humans had divorce.

Of course, Zach never thought about mates or mating as much until he came to this fucking little town in the middle of nowhere. All because of her. A crazy woman who apparently couldn't drive very well and insisted on hanging around other crazy women. Plus, it really didn't help she wanted him. Boy, did she want him. He could practically hear her clit twitching from where he stood. But what pissed him off was that his dick kept getting hard every time he saw her. Every time he thought about her. What the hell was that anyway?

Even thinking about seeing her this morning, before he caught sight of her truck, his dick was rock solid. That was unacceptable. He didn't want any woman to have that much control over him. Especially Sara Morrighan.

He knew he couldn't get attached to her. He wouldn't. Just turn her and go. He had plans to make and a Pack to protect. No time to get involved with some nutty girl whose grandmother probably damaged her more than the Pride that scarred her face and body.

The problem was it sometimes took years to turn someone. To get them to face their true selves. It took years before they felt that surge of power, years before they could shift at will and hunt with the Pack. But, of course, that's what Casey wanted. For a girl who wouldn't be comfortable with who she was for quite awhile to distract his dumb ass. Twenty-eight years was a very long time to be completely oblivious to who and what you really are.

Zach's cell phone went off. He looked at the caller ID and sighed. Casey. "Yeah?"

"Hey, Zach. It's Casey." Dumb bitch. She knew they all had caller ID. "Yeah?"

"I need you to pick up Julie's bike from the shop today."

Yeah, of course she did. "Okay."

"Great!" She hung up.

Zach shut his phone off. "Gotta pick up Julie's bike. Wanna come?"

Before Conall could answer his cell phone went off. Conall looked at the caller ID, smiled, and answered. "This is Conall. Yeah. Okay." He hung up. "Can't."

"That was Casey, wasn't it?"

Conall shrugged. "Sorry, Zach. She wants me to help out at the site."

Zach sighed again. "Sure she does."

Great. Now he had to go deal with Sara and that old wolf Marrec. Well, maybe Sara was on her own.

Alone with Sara...yup. His dick just went hard again. He would have to do something about that. It was really starting to piss him off.

Chapter Six

"You are going to that party tomorrow, aren't you?"

Sara looked up from her chopper magazine and glared at her boss. He sat on the other side of the counter polishing off his chicken fried rice and beef with mushrooms like he hadn't eaten in three days. The coolest thing about working for Marrec, though...every day she worked at the shop, she never had to pay for food. "Maybe."

"Why maybe? Why not yes?"

"Jesus, Marrec. What is the big deal? It's a freakin' party. Not the prom." Thank God. Her prom turned ugly right quick with Miki and Angelina starting that brawl and all. Talk about a long night in jail.

"You know I'm worried about you, right?"

Of course he was worried about her. Marrec always worried about her. You'd think the man didn't have six kids of his own and more grandkids than Sara cared to think about. And his protective attitude seemed to trickle down to his whole family and—because everyone respected the old coot—right through the entire town. They all protected her. Like it was their job or something.

"Why would you be worried? Could my life be any quieter? I mean, nothing has changed for me in like ten years. Actually, I think Lynette's death has been the most exciting time I've had in awhile." Not a lot of wakes turn into a party unless you were in New Orleans, but everyone hated her grandmother so it wasn't really a huge surprise. "So why you should worry about me, I don't know."

"Because. You deserve more than what your grandmother convinced you you deserved."

Sara rolled her eyes, shoving the chicken chow mein away from her. Maybe it was her annoyance at this ridiculous conversation, but the smell had started to seriously bother her. "Come on, Marrec. What exactly are you expecting for me? That my two years of community college will lead to a high life of big business? Or maybe now I can go for that medical degree."

"You are such a smart ass."

"No. I'm a realist. Always have been. I have no delusions. Never could afford them. I just wish everybody would stop worrying about me. You know, I can take care of myself."

Marrec grunted as he closed the lid on his empty container. "Yes, yes. We all know how scary dangerous you can be."

"You don't have to be so sarcastic about it." Okay. So maybe Miki and Angelina were ten times scarier than she was, but she had her dangerous moments. Ask anyone who'd been around her when she'd been drinking.

"Just do me a favor, okay?" Marrec stood up. "Go to the party. Meet the people there."

Frowning, Sara shook her head. Usually Marrec went out of his way to get between her and a pack of bikers. Now he wanted to toss her into their laps. Strange. Very, very strange.

"Look, I'm going. Okay? So stop askin' me."

"Good." Marrec shoved his empty containers across the counter to her. "Thanks."

She watched the ornery old bastard head to the back of the store. "I guess I'm taking out the trash?"

"Yup. Ya are."

Grumbling, Sara took her and Marrec's lunch containers outside and tossed them in the Dumpster next to the shop.

"Is that you, Sara?" she heard Jake, from Jake's Auto, yell over the six-foot-high wall separating Marrec's shop from his.

"Yup."

"Randy's coming over."

"Randy. Randy. Randy," she chanted in a high-pitched voice as a one-hundred-pound red-nosed pit bull came around the corner. His leash and pinch collar still attached, although Sara never had to use them. His tongue hanging out, he trotted over to her and waited for his daily hello.

As much as it hurt, Sara crouched low beside him. "Is this my Randy? Is this my good boy?" She rubbed her hands along his flank. He growled and lay down on the concrete on his side. She continued to rub his thigh and back. "Who's my pretty boy? Who's my special guy?" Randy, as always, rolled over onto his back and Sara rubbed his belly, continuing to ignore the growing pain in her leg. She couldn't disappoint Randy. "Who's my good boy?"

"So, can I be next?"

Sara gasped in surprise at Zach's voice, but she needed to get that under control. She hated the show of weakness.

"Um—" was all that came out before sweet, lovable Randy jumped up and charged straight at Zach, his teeth bared. Sara caught the leash and yanked Randy back, the dog's jaws snapping shut mere inches from Zach's face. But Zach didn't move. He didn't even flinch. In fact, he stared at Randy as if unimpressed with the sight of the one-hundred-pound dog trying to turn him into a midday meal.

Sara, still keeping a strong grip on the leash, turned her head to yell over the wall, "Jake! I need you!" She heard a vicious snarl and when she turned back, Randy had backed off, tail between his legs.

He ran behind Sara—whimpering.

She looked at Zach who stood in the same position he had been in five seconds before. Leaning against the wall, his arms crossed in front of his chest, completely relaxed.

"What did you do to him?"

"Not a thing."

Jake came around the corner. "What in hell…"

"You better take him, Jake." Sara handed over the leash.

Jake took it, but didn't leave immediately. "You sure y'all okay?" He sized Zach up with narrowed eyes. "Randy don't usually act like this, 'cept when he don't like somebody."

"I'm fine. Really. Thanks, Jake."

Jake gave Zach one more nasty look, and dragged the whimpering Randy back around the concrete wall.

"I've never seen Randy act like that." She regarded Zach closely. "He really hated you."

"But I'm so charming."

Sara gave a short laugh. "Yeah. Right." She headed back to the store. "So, why are you here?"

"Julie's new bike. I need to get it."

"Well, then, come on."

ରେ ରେ ରେ

Zach caught her scent as soon as he'd gotten out of the pickup truck the Pack brought with them for hauling stuff around. He followed it to the side of the shop, but never expected to find her lathering up some pit bull. Shamelessly, in fact.

Who's my good boy? Was she kidding? Hell, he could be her good boy. Her *very* good boy. Or her very bad one.

As he watched her tight ass move into the store, he knew one of Marrec's Pack—*Jake, right?*—watched him. Zach turned and snarled at the nosy bastard, sending that weak-willed pit bull whimpering for safety and causing Jake's eyes to glance away.

When Zach turned around, Sara stared at him. "Did you just...snarl?"

"I have a cough."

"A snarling cough?"

"Something like that."

Looking truly distrusting, Sara went into the store and Zach followed behind her. "*Marrec!*" Sara screamed into the back. "Someone's here to pick up that girl's bike!"

"Gimme ten minutes!" Marrec yelled back.

As she perched herself on the stool behind the counter, she caught Zach's expression. "What?"

"Are you always so loud?"

"You'd be amazed."

Zach smiled. "Kind of a screamer?"

She blushed and rolled her eyes. "Cute."

He liked it when she blushed—it looked good on her.

Zach leaned against the glass case. "You and your friends are definitely coming to the party, right?"

Before Sara could answer, Marrec yelled from the back, "Yes, she is!"

"He doesn't think I get out enough," Sara muttered.

"Do you?"

"Not lately. Death in the family a few months back."

"I'm sorry."

"Don't be. No one else is." Sara winced. "Okay. That was bitchy. Forget I said that. I mean, she wasn't that bad."

"Who?" Although he already knew.

"My grandmother. She raised me...sort of. Died about six months back. The last few months I've been busy sorting out all her finances and business. I just finished cleaning out her house a few weeks ago...well, I guess it's my house now."

"Find anything cool? When my father died, my mom and I found a ton of cool stuff at their place."

"Some. Had to give a lot of it back to the government, though."

Zach frowned. "Give what back to the government? Money?"

"No." She started counting off on her fingers. "The M-16. The armor-piercing ammo. The rocket launcher. The grenades."

"Your grandmother had a rocket launcher?"

Sara chuckled. "Apparently she was expecting some kind of attack. She was extremely paranoid. I don't even know where she got that shit from. And you know what? I don't wanna know."

No wonder the Pride waited until the old bitch died. Even they couldn't handle a full-on assault from military weapons. Yates hadn't been kidding— that old woman had been truly dangerous.

"Did you get any money for that stuff?"

"No. I just wanted it gone. I have my daddy's old shotgun, which I use for huntin'. And Miki and Angelina gave me a pump-action shotgun couple of years back for," she smiled while making air quotes with her fingers, "'basic home defense'. So, I don't need much more than that."

"You a good shot?"

"I'm okay. Miki's better. I've seen her nail a buck at two-hundred feet. Right between the eyes."

"That's a lovely story. Learn that in etiquette school?"

"*Texas* etiquette school."

He liked that too. She didn't shrink away from his teasing or get insulted. She rolled with it.

"You work here long?" He looked around the impressive store. Marrec did some amazing work. There were custom-made bikes here he'd seen on the pages of some of his chopper magazines. They weren't merely bikes. They were pieces of art.

"Since I was fourteen. Marrec said it would keep me off the streets."

Zach glanced out the window to what had to be the quietest town he'd ever been in. "Big gang problem around here? Lots of cow jacking?"

"We have all sorts pass through our little town, thank you very much. Bikers. Cowboys. The always dangerous rodeo clowns."

"Rodeo clowns?"

"Don't ask."

Zach shrugged. "I don't want to know."

"Any other condescending questions about my town?"

"Oh, I'm not being condescending. I'm very interested in your tiny little town, with its tiny little people. I bet you guys even have a movie theater."

Sara barked out a laugh. "You certainly are a charmer."

"So I've been told."

"By who? Your mother?"

"She does adore her son." He looked out the window again. "I thought there'd be desert. Coyotes. Clint Eastwood."

"You're in Hill Country. We have rivers, canyons and forests. You want desert, you need to hit the Panhandle."

Zach leaned across the counter and smiled at her. "You'll have to show me around some time."

"I have been known to go off alone with strange bikers," she responded sarcastically. "It's a thing I do. Like eating glass."

"Does this mean you won't go out with me tonight?" *Wait. Why are you asking her out?* Probably because she was a major piece of ass and looked like she could suck a golf ball through a hose.

"No. That means I won't be showing you around my town."

"So you will go out with me tonight." He didn't phrase that as a question. He didn't want her to think it was an option.

That didn't seem to mean much to her, though, as she smirked and said, "I'm not going out with you."

"Why?"

"Because I have sense."

He heard the front door open and she frowned.

"Oh, shit," she muttered under her breath.

"Well, hello, all."

Angelina walked up to the counter, a brown paper bag in her hand. "I'm not interrupting anything, am I?"

"He's here to pick up that girl's bike."

"The one who crashed?" Angelina glanced at Zach. "How is she doing anyway?"

"Right as rain."

"That's interesting," Angelina said, thoughtful. "She's a mighty fast healer."

"That she is."

Angelina turned back to Sara. "I came to drop this off. Didn't want Miki to see." Sara took the paper bag and looked inside.

"Christ!" She slammed the bag shut and tossed it into an open backpack behind her. "I hate you."

"Just watching out for my friends." Angelina turned and strode out of the store. "See ya at the party, Zach."

"Bye." He didn't turn around, too busy staring at the blush creeping up Sara's neck and straight to her hairline. "You okay?"

"Fine," she bit out way too quickly. "Just fine."

Zach wasn't buying it. "Can I see what's in the bag?"

"No!" She almost yelled it. "Tampons."

"I'm ready," Marrec called from his workshop. "Send him back."

"You better go." She tried to shoo him from the room.

"You know," Zach moved toward the workshop entrance, "when my sister and I were teenagers, she always threw out 'tampon' when she didn't want Dad to see our bag of pot. But you and your friends seem amazingly straight edge to me. So it makes me wonder…what's really in that bag?"

Zach backed into the workshop as Sara's face turned a darker crimson. Then he hit a wall and turned around to find that wall was actually Marrec.

"Having fun?" Marrec asked, his arms folded across what might be a normal chest for a bear. The man was short but powerfully built. Red wolves were always a little "stunty", though.

"Loads."

"You know her father died when she was very young."

Of course he did. That's why they were here in the first place.

"And I kind of took his place. She's as close to me as any of my daughters. And I'll kill any man who fucks with her."

Zach wondered if Marrec already had. "Good to know."

Once Zach disappeared in the back, Sara shoved the bag filled with boxes—and boxes!—of condoms into her backpack. She was going to kill Angelina when she saw her.

She had one friend throwing condoms at her and the other telling her men were nothing but trouble. But as much shit as the three of them talked, they probably knew less about men than anyone on the planet. They all had their own ways of keeping people at bay. Miki had her intense distrust of…well, *everyone*. Angelina had her fortress of ice. And Sara had her armor. They'd all destroyed potential relationships in record time and without much regret. And although they never discussed it, none of them ever really believed they'd find true love or romance or any of that other crap.

So why did Sara feel like Zach was somehow different? What was it about him that spoke to her on some other level the few men she'd had in her oh-so-tame past never could? Why did she itch to touch his skin? To feel him touch her? What was it about this man that made her feel like she'd been waiting her entire life for him to come walking through her door?

What was it about this man that made her want to punch him right in the forehead?

Marrec moved over to the bike he'd readied for Julie.

Zach kicked the door to the workshop closed, ensuring Sara couldn't hear the conversation. "I have a question."

Marrec leaned against the bike, his arms again crossed in front of his chest. "Why didn't I turn her myself?"

"It would make sense."

"Her grandmother. The craziest bitch I've ever met on two feet or four. Did Sara tell you what she found in her house when she cleaned it out?"

Zach nodded. "Yeah. She did."

"When my oldest boy showed interest in Sara, she set my car on fire. She said after that it would be my house."

Zach felt a growing sense of horror for this woman's self-hatred. He couldn't imagine his life without the Pack. Without being who he was.

"If only she would have shifted, I would have snapped her neck. But I wasn't going to kill her as human."

Zach didn't blame him. Kill one of them as human, they stayed human. Kill them as beast and they stayed beast. In the end, much easier to explain the dead animal on your territory to the cops.

"So, I figured I'd wait until the old bitch died on her own. I just didn't know she'd take so long to do it."

"She's in a lot of pain, you know."

Marrec sighed. A sad one from deep inside his chest. "I know. And her aggression is getting worse, too." Marrec grabbed a stack of papers off the counter behind the bike. "To be honest, I think it's poison." He handed the papers to Zach.

"Poison?"

"The Withell Pride is known for dipping their claws in poison. Prolongs the agony."

"That's very human of them," Zach noted with disgust.

"But I can't get her near a doctor. Her grandmother made sure of that. The girl's terrified of anything medical."

Zach flipped through the bill of sale and other paperwork Marrec handed him. "What would she need done?"

"It's a little barbaric…she'd have to be bled. But several of the docs at the hospital are part of my Pack so it wouldn't be a problem." Marrec shook his head. "But not until she knows who and what she is. If we just turn her,

I'm afraid of what she'll do. Maybe I'll talk with Yates about it. About the timing."

Zach nodded, keeping his expression purposely blank. "Sure. Whatever."

Chapter Seven

Sara barely moved back in time as a biker from the next town stepped in front of her so he could talk to Angie.

"Uh…excuse me?" she asked, even while laughing.

He looked at her like she'd just appeared out of thin air. "Oh. Hey, Sara. Sorry. Didn't see ya there."

"Yeah. At six feet, I am so small and undetectable."

"Huh?"

Angie reached around and grabbed hold of the sleeve of Sara's leather jacket. "Excuse us." Angie dragged her over to the bar.

"You and those legs, Santiago," Sara teased, marveling at how only Angie could make the tacky gold short skirt she wore look classy rather than slutty.

"Shut up." Angie stepped up to the bar, ignoring the men staring at her, plotting their move in the hopes of getting two seconds of her time. She knocked on the bar with her knuckles. "Excuse me. Bar slut?"

Miki didn't even turn away from the three regulars she was helping as she reached back with one arm and gave Angie the finger.

"How rude!"

"Leave her alone." Sara laughed while glancing around the club. Packed but with a lot more unknown faces then she'd seen in a long time.

"Who are all these people?"

"Must be here for tomorrow's rave." And then Angie threw her arms up in the air and "woo-hoo'd" for the benefit of everyone.

"Jeez, Ang. We're not even there yet and you're already grooving."

"You know me. I do always love a good party."

Miki stepped in front of them. "All right. What do you bitches want?"

"Oh, very nice. Does Skelly know you're so rude to your customers?"

"You're not customers. You're family. I can talk to you anyway I damn well want to. So you two want something or are you here simply to annoy me?"

"Both."

Miki looked at Sara. "What'cha want?"

"A shot of te—"

"Don't even think about saying tequila to me," Miki cut in. "I'm not picking your fat ass off the floor yet again."

Sara's eyes narrowed. "My ass is not fat."

"Are you happy in your fantasy world, sweetie?" Angie asked, her arm around Sara's shoulders. "Are your tits small there, too?" Angie ducked when Sara jokingly raised her fist.

Laughing, Angie turned to Miki. "You have any chardonnay?"

Miki rolled her eyes, grabbed two Heinekens out of the fridge behind her, popped the tops, and slammed them in front of her friends. "Now don't bother me."

"Isn't she like a breath of fresh air?"

Sara shook her head. "No. Not really."

ର ର ର

God, he was getting pathetic. He caught her scent as soon as she walked into the club and his entire body tightened in lust. What was happening? Zach Sheridan didn't get all bunged up over women. Ever. It was not in his nature. There were only two women he took special interest in protecting or caring about and one he called "Mom" the other he called "shithead" or "baby sis".

Sara didn't notice him, but that didn't surprise him. That grandmother of hers made sure Sara was completely oblivious to the power buried inside that sweet body.

She sat at the bar knocking back a beer in a worn leather biker jacket three times too big for her. Clearly a man's jacket. Zach scowled when he allowed himself to wonder if that jacket belonged to some asshole. Some asshole other than him, that is. He didn't like the thought. Even as he fought it, he didn't like to think for a second Sara might be getting down and as dirty as he'd been daydreaming about lately with some scumbag. Some scumbag other than him, that is.

The music changed into good trance and a guy invited Angie to join him on the dance floor. With a wink at Sara, she followed behind him. The Mouth, as he liked to call the current object of Conall's lust, was up to her eyes in patrons, which left Sara sitting there by herself. It was like she didn't exist to these people. How could they miss her? The males of his Pack noticed her and if it weren't for him, they'd be sniffing around her right now. But the locals and the bikers acted like she was part of the wallpaper. What idiots.

Still, Sara didn't look upset. Instead, she sat on the barstool, drinking her beer and watching everything around her. Absorbing. That's what she did. No one else may realize it, but Sara had the hard, cold eyes of a predator. And it turned Zach on something fierce.

Sara let the trance music flow through her, her head moving to the beat as she spun her stool around. The music dropped and she raised her arms in the air, howling out a "woo-hoo" right along with the entire crowd as the music hovered right "there".

Oh, yeah, this DJ was awesome. The beat swung back up and the crowd roared in appreciation.

Yeah. This is what she loved. When the music took her away. Even for a little while. For a few moments, she forgot the pain, her grandmother and her less-than-thrilling life. She forgot it all while letting that beat move through her.

Someone sat next to her and she glanced to her left, expecting to see Angie. Instead, she saw him. Leaning back against the bar, his elbows resting on the polished wood, and his legs stretched out in front of him and crossed at the ankles. The man seemed to have an array of black, unknown-band T-shirts, blue jeans that fit his superb ass perfectly, and biker boots. He didn't wear much else and, God in heaven, he really didn't need to.

"Thought you weren't going out tonight," he said, raising his voice enough so she could hear him over the music but not enough for her to consider the yelling a threat.

"That's not what I said," she responded. "I said I wasn't going out tonight with you."

"And why was that again?"

"Cause I don't like you."

He snorted, it was sort of like a laugh, and went back to watching the crowd.

Christ, the man was irritating. Cute and hot and irritating.

She was seconds away from asking him why the hell he was even talking to her when a flash of gold dragged her eyes back to the dance floor. Sure enough, Angie had just stumbled back from two guys about to gut each other over her. It wouldn't be the first time. Men, especially bikers, loved to fight over Angie. Of course, the one who got her could never keep her. But no point in telling them that. They saw Angie in all her cute, gold outfits and sexy, way overpriced shoes and thought they could handle her.

When they ended up in the ER, the doctors desperately trying to figure out how to stop the bleeding, those same guys always seemed so surprised.

Sara knocked against the bar with her knuckles, catching Miki's attention.

"Angie alert."

Miki looked out over the dance floor and growled.

"Leon!" she yelled, and the bouncer was there in an instant with one of the new trainees. They grabbed hold of the men and Sara barely caught Miki in time, trying to dive over the bar with her baseball bat firmly in hand.

"Don't even think about it, Kendrick."

The two bouncers picked the fighting men off the floor and dragged them to the exit.

"Dammit, Morrighan!" Miki, grinning, slid back off the bar. "I could have taken at least one of them out and it would have been totally legal this time." She slipped the bat back to its hiding place under the bar at the same time she caught sight of Zach. "What's he doing here?"

Sara shrugged. "I don't know." Sara looked at Zach. "What are you doing here?"

"Enjoying the wonder that is Texas."

Trying hard not to laugh, Sara said to Miki, "He's learning to love our mighty state."

Miki rolled her eyes. "Whatever."

And then he was there. The big blond stalker. He smiled at Miki. "Hi."

She didn't even try and fake that particular conversation. Instead, Miki yelled, "Break!" and then disappeared into the back room, slamming the door behind her.

The blond frowned in confusion and gave his order to the other bartender.

"Fun friends."

Sara turned and faced Zach. "If I didn't know better I'd swear that was sarcasm I just heard."

"Me? Sarcastic? That's crazy talk."

"Then you fit in perfectly around here."

Zach motioned to the beer in her hand. "Want another one?" Okay, was he buying her a drink or just buying her a drink? *Hhhhm. This is a new level of idiotic questions, Morrighan.*

But before she could turn him down or shove her tongue down his throat, he said, "Behind you."

"What?"

He didn't repeat himself. Just grabbed hold of her jacket and yanked her over to him. Her body slammed up against his, her breasts pressing into his hard chest. She gasped in surprise and sexual awareness. Oh, yeah, this guy felt good! Still, that didn't mean he could go around grabbing her. Before she could tell him to get his big paws off her fat ass, something slammed into her from behind, shoving her closer to Zach. At this point, if she were any closer, they'd be fucking.

Sara's eyes stayed locked on Zach's rich hazel ones. No one had ever looked at her like this. Like they could eat her alive.

For a split second she thought he might actually try and kiss her—and she didn't know whether she'd kiss him back or stab him in the face—but his next comment took her by surprise.

"Nice jacket."

"Uh…" Sara looked down at the worn and very loved jacket she wore as often as she could. "Thanks?"

"Where'd you get it from?"

That was none of his goddamn business, but she heard herself answering before she could stop herself. "It was my dad's."

His hazel eyes searched hers like he was trying to figure out if she were lying. Definitely not a guy who trusted a lot of women.

After several moments, he muttered, "Good."

Before she could deal with why that might be good and why the hell did he care about her wardrobe and why did he keep looking at her like steak tar tar; the chanting behind her picked up volume and her eyes widened in panic.

"Get her! Get her!"

Oh, Lord!

Sara pulled away from Zach and spun around. Two women viciously fought each other and Sara leaned forward, trying to get a good look.

"You thought it was me, didn't you?"

Standing up straight, Sara couldn't believe the overwhelming relief coursing through her when she realized Angie sat on the stool beside her and not in the middle of the bar fight.

"No. Of course not," she lied. "I was being nosy is all."

"Lying heifer." Angie sipped her beer and crossed her legs. Audible groans came from the men around her.

"So, Morrighan, having fun?"

Sara stared at her friend until she realized Angie kept motioning at Zach…and that Zach had noticed.

"Jesus Christ!" She grabbed Angie's arm and dragged her around the bar and into the back. Not surprisingly, Miki sat on a box of liquor reading a book.

"What's going on?" she asked while standing and walking over to them.

"I swear, Santiago! You are an idiot!"

"I'm only trying to help you along. The guy is all over you and you need to let him know you're interested before some other biker slut, such as yourself, snaps him up with a well-timed blow job."

"I'm not interested. I'm not a biker slut. And eeewww."

"You so *are* interested."

"He's on the List," Miki chimed in.

Angie shoved Miki by her shoulder. "Shut up."

"Don't shove me," Miki snapped, shoving Angie back.

As the ugly slap fight ensued, Sara went back out into the bar.

Zach watched her limp back into the bar. The two women who had been fighting—and gave him the perfect excuse to drag Sara's amazingly delicious body right into his—had been dragged out by the bouncers.

To his surprise, she limped back to the stool next to him and slid back on it. He barely caught his growl in time when he thought about her doing the same move to his face.

"Everything okay?" Zach asked.

Sara shrugged. "Just another night at Skelly's. Nothing to worry your pretty, big, fat head about."

It took a lot not to laugh. For a girl raised as human, she was damn funny when she wanted to be.

He held her beer out to her. "Here."

She looked down at it like it had a snake wrapped around it. "You want me to drink that?"

"What? Too warm?"

She snorted. "Sorry. I think I'll avoid taking opened but unattended bottles of beer from guys I barely know."

After a moment of being insulted, Zach realized if this was his sister, he'd tear her ass up if she took a bottle of beer from a near stranger. Even with her heightened senses, it was a dumb fucking move.

Sara had common sense, too. Dammit! He needed to find some flaws with this chick soon or he was going to get in way over his head.

She ordered a fresh beer from the bartender and motioned to Zach. "He'll pay for it."

"I will?"

Tilting the bottle toward her full lips, she grinned. "Yeah. You will."

"And why is that exactly?"

Still grinning and now drinking, she shrugged. He was more than ready to take this discussion to the bathroom where he could fuck the answer out of her, but his cell phone went off.

"Yeah?" he barked into the phone, his eyes locked on her long, exposed throat and all the smooth skin he wanted to taste with his tongue as she swigged back that beer.

"Zach. It's Julie. We need you back here. Problem with a few of the vendors and Yates is about to go feral."

Zach sighed. There went his bathroom plans. "Yeah. Yeah. I'll take care of it." He closed his phone.

She placed the beer bottle back on the bar as her tongue darted out and licked up a drop of liquid from her bottom lip. Zach balled his free hand into a fist and let the tips of his claws peek out enough to dig into his flesh and cause enough pain to distract him from grabbing the woman, bending her over the bar, and fucking her within an inch of her life. "I gotta go back," he managed to grumble. "Problems with vendors at the site for tomorrow."

"Wow." She smirked. "How much I really don't care."

He gave a low growl. "You'll be there tomorrow, right?" Eesh. He made that sound like an order to be on time for a court date.

"That's the plan."

"Good."

"Doesn't mean I need to see your ass there, though."

Damn but the woman played with fire.

Stepping in front of her, Zach stared down into her pretty face. For a really long time he stared at her and Sara stared back. She didn't flinch. She didn't hide. She didn't back down at all. *Nice.*

"I'll see you tomorrow," he finally said.

With heavy sarcasm, she responded, "I'm all breathless with anticipation. Can't ya tell?"

Zach studied her body, examining her from head to foot and back again. Finally his eyes locked on hers and he said, "You will be."

Then he walked out, the rest of the Pack instinctively following him.

Chapter Eight

"Dude, I made out like gangbusters tonight!" Miki pulled a healthy wad of cash out of her pocket and flashed it at her friends while Angie jumped into the cab and closed the truck door.

"And what are we planning to do with all that cash?"

"Computer memory, thank you very much."

Angie sighed. "What do you need computer memory for?"

"Because she wants to see if she misses that interrogation room and…what was that guy's name again, Ang?"

"Agent Jones?"

"You two are never going to let me forget *that* are you?"

"No," they barked in unison.

It was nearly four in the morning, but Sara and Angie stayed because they didn't want to leave poor Miki. The big blond left when Zach left but Miki kept worrying he'd come back. To be honest, Sara didn't know what Miki was so concerned about. The guy was adorable and just a big 'ol teddy bear. But Miki could convince herself of pretty much anything when she set her mind to it. No point in fighting her on it.

Sara dropped off Angie first. The woman's house was big and gorgeous. Everything perfectly placed and designed…and all Angie did there was sleep.

If you were looking for Angie you were more likely to find her at Sara's house or Miki's apartment.

"Sara—" Miki began.

"We're going, Miki. We are going to this rave and I don't want to discuss this anymore."

There was no way she wasn't going to the rave. Not after the last thing Zach said to her. The mere thought of those words had her nipples tightening under her Harley T-shirt and part of her really wanted to squirm. Probably a bad idea. Miki would definitely notice squirming.

"Fine!"

Sara chuckled. "I swear, you are like a dog with a bone."

"I'm only trying to prevent our life stories from being re-told on *America's Most Wanted*." Miki's voice dropped several octaves. "But little did these innocent women know that this rave would be their last...*ever.*"

Her chuckle turning into a full-blown guffaw, Sara worked hard to keep her focus on the road. "Cut it out! We'll be fine. Marrec gave his word, remember?"

"Yeah. That still bothers me. When has Marrec ever trusted anybody from outside this town? Mister Why Are You On My Territory."

"I don't know. But I trust Marrec and he trusts them. We'll be fine. And if you don't learn to relax you're going to become one of those cranky old people the neighborhood kids throw rocks at."

Sara stopped her truck in front of Miki's apartment complex. "So please, do us all a favor before Angie rips your tits off...chill out."

"Fine. Whatever." Miki pushed the passenger door open but stopped before stepping out. She looked over her shoulder at Sara. "Are you okay?"

"Yeah. Why?"

Miki shrugged her small shoulders. "No reason. But you know if you need anything or whatever, I'm right here. So's Angie."

"Kendrick, what are you talking about?"

With a shake of her head, Miki stepped out of the truck. "Nothin'. I'll talk to you tomorrow."

"You mean today, don't you?"

"Whatever." Miki smiled and slammed the truck door closed. She waved and Sara waited until she saw Miki go up the stairs, into her apartment, and turn the inside light on. Their signal that Miki had checked her tiny apartment and found no serial rapist hiding in any corners.

Sara headed home, not even bothering to turn the radio on. She'd felt it as soon as she arrived at Miki's place. The first streaks of pain heralding one of her recent spate of "episodes". Pain so bad some days, she wasn't sure how she functioned. And sometimes, she didn't function. Instead she'd find herself face down on her kitchen floor or tangled up in her clothes in the back of her closet. The episodes had been getting worse and more frequent, but no way in hell was she going to tell Miki and Angie about it.

So focused on the road and getting back to her house before the pain became too much, Sara didn't even realize something was following her until that something hit her truck with a loud "bang!"

She didn't stop driving. Miki had trained them well on serial killer M.O. But Sara looked in her rear view and that's when she blinked in confusion. Cats. Two big cats in her rear view, racing after her. She frowned. Still dark out and only her taillights to guide her—one still busted since she hadn't been able to afford to fix it—and Sara really couldn't be sure she saw what she saw. They moved like cats, though. But she couldn't remember seeing mountain lions around these parts in the entire twenty years she'd lived here. And she'd gone hunting many, many times during those years. She never saw the kind of paw prints or markings indicating cats in the area. When she thought about it, not even stray house cats.

Add in that those things looked really *huge* for mountain lions…

A voice in the back of Sara's mind kept telling her something was seriously wrong, but Sara didn't know what and she wasn't sure she wanted to know. Instead, she pressed on the gas and booked it home. She had to admit it, she was scared. Seeing those things running behind her truck like they wanted nothing more than to use her bones to pick their teeth clean of her remains had her adrenaline pulsing fast and hot through her system.

Sara's truck tore down the deserted highway to her house. Tires squealed as she made a wild turn onto the dirt road leading home. She came to a screeching halt in front of her house and sat several long seconds in her truck trying to breathe and to see if anything was still gunning for her. She couldn't see anything. Nothing followed her.

Hands shaking, she pushed open the door to her truck and stepped out. As soon as her bad leg touched the ground, Sara went down with a scream. Pain so intense tears rushed to her eyes, ripped through her body completely crippling her. She hit the ground hard, her hands gripping her leg. She gritted her teeth together, trying not to scream again, trying not to show weakness.

She didn't show weakness. Not if she could help it. When her grandmother still lived, showing weakness would only invite a painful lesson on what pain really was. So Sara learned not to show her pain. Learned not to show how much she hurt. But this pain…this was worse than anything she'd ever experienced before.

Desperate and scared, no longer caring about mountain lions or anything else but herself, Sara used every ounce of strength she possessed to drag herself up using her truck door. She kept her wounded leg off the ground and made the long, painful way back to her house using the hood of her truck as a crutch. She moved around until she leaned against the side of the truck facing her front porch. Knowing she wouldn't be able to make the very few steps from truck to porch, Sara pushed herself off and landed face down on the stairs.

Somehow, Sara dragged herself up those stairs and to her front door. She managed to pull out her keys, but before she could even try to raise herself up to get the key in the lock, another pain tore through her, her entire body thrown into a brutal spasm. The scream she couldn't help but release rang out through the trees surrounding her house.

Then absolutely everything went black.

ભ ભ ભ

Zach woke up when Kelly hit him in the head with her paw. Yawning, he rolled over and watched his Pack take down a deer for breakfast. He thought about joining them, but he was too busy mentally kicking himself in the ass. Exactly why did he grab Sara last night? And what was his obsession over that goddamn leather jacket? His relief at hearing it once belonged to her dad nearly made him physically ill.

I'm such an idiot.

"Hey."

Looking up at Conall, "What?" Conall learned long ago Zach was not a morning person. So he never expected civil behavior.

"I think Pride was in Marrec's territory last night."

Zach snarled and pushed himself to his feet. "And?"

"And nothing. I caught the scent when I was heading back from town in the truck. Just thought you'd want to know."

"Shit."

"What?"

"I better check on her," Zach sighed.

"Because checking on Sara's your job now?"

Zach stared at the ground, his hands on his hips. "What time is it?"

"About eleven."

"And what's the rule?"

"Don't even think about speaking to you until noon."

"Then why are you testing me?"

"Cause it's fun to watch you turn that certain color of angry red."

℃ ℃ ℃

It was the wet nose in her ear that woke her up. The pain had receded to its normal, dull ache and now Sara could see straight. Using her hands, she pushed the top half of her body up and looked around.

"Good Lord, I passed out on my porch."

At least this time it wasn't cause she was drunk off her ass or in a fistfight.

A low growl from off to her left caught Sara's attention and held it. She looked over and a brown-eyed wolf stared back at her.

She felt a long wet tongue against a spot on her back where her jacket and T-shirt rode up when she fell. Glancing over her shoulder, she saw another wolf. Big, beautiful, and definitely a predator based on the size of those fangs.

There were more, too. Lots more. The wolves from the woods. The ones she howled to every night. They were on her porch, in front of her porch, on the hood of her truck.

Sara worked really hard trying not to panic and thanked God Miki wasn't around. Her screaming would have caused all sorts of problems.

Suddenly, Sara realized something—they weren't trying to hurt her. Actually, except for two or three watching her, they didn't seem too interested in her at all now that she'd started moving on her own.

They'd come to protect her.

Sitting up with her all night while she lay passed out on her front porch, watching over her.

She could be wrong—she wasn't exactly a scholar like Miki—but she was relatively positive that wasn't normal wolf behavior.

Once Sara pulled herself into a sitting position, they trotted off. No "Hope you're okay" licks or friendly paw pats on the shoulder. Now that she could care for herself, they left.

"Is it my imagination or is my life getting really weird?" she asked no on in particular.

Deciding not to think about it, Sara pushed herself to her feet and stretched. She almost sighed in relief. Back to her normal, *manageable* pain. Who knew she'd prefer that to whatever she'd endured last night?

No. Not a good idea to think about it too much. She'd only panic and make it worse.

Limping to her front door, she unlocked it and pushed it open. She was about to step in when she froze, instinctively knowing something watched her.

Sara looked over her shoulder and saw him. The biggest goddamn wolf she'd ever seen. He stood at the edge of the trees, far away from her. She knew if he charged her, she'd be able to get into her house in time. So she let herself stare back at him.

A big wolf with black fur and he watched her like he owned her.

Sara shook her head at that extremely disturbing thought.

No. No. She was not going to let the pain make her lose her mind. She wouldn't stand for it. Her grandmother was crazy, she absolutely refused to be crazy too.

A quick glance back and she realized the wolf had walked off with the others. Letting out a deep sigh and really concerned her nipples were hard— *it's just the fear, sweetie. Nothing to panic about. It's just the fear*—Sara stepped into her house and shut the door.

Chapter Nine

"Ever hunt mountain lion around here, Marrec?"

Marrec grinned at Sara's question, his big hand using a soft cloth to carefully wipe down the chrome on one of his newest creations. "Around here, nah. But I've hunted them a time or two other places. Why?"

Sara kept the stack of bills in her lap, her fingers moving through them quickly. She needed to finish settling a few accounts before she could leave and get ready for that night's party.

Without looking up from her paperwork, "No reason. Just thought I saw a couple last night."

"How many?"

"There it is." Sara gripped the receipt in her hand, relieved to have found it. "I couldn't find this guy's paper—ow!"

Startled, Sara stared at the familiar hand gripping her wrist. "What is your damage?"

"Answer my question."

She'd always been close to Marrec. He'd taken care of her during those "juvenile delinquent" years when no other adult really had. The man had always been protective of her, but in the last week he'd been getting more and more weird. And she was getting damn tired of it.

"Let me go."

Blinking, like he'd only just realized he gripped her like she was trying to steal his family fortune, he released her arm.

"Sorry."

Sara separated the needed paperwork from all the others and put the rest in a file. "Marrec, are you okay?"

"Yeah. Yeah. I'm fine. Just getting old, I guess."

"Here." She handed him the paperwork. "Are you sure you don't want me to wait around for this guy to show up?"

"No. You go. Have a good time. And, Sara, be careful."

"Aren't I always?"

"Yeah. But you'll have those two nutcases with you. Sometimes you're so busy trying to prevent them from doing something stupid, you end up in the middle of a shit storm. I'd rather no more late-night calls from deputies if you can help it."

"You act like that happened a lot. Six...seven times top."

Sara grinned and Marrec laughed and shook his head. "Go. I'll see you tomorrow."

Slipping on her leather jacket, "Not too early, though."

With a snort, Marrec barked back, "When the hell have you ever been early for anything, Sara Morrighan?"

CR CR CR

The arguing about clothes began as soon as Sara picked Miki and Angelina up that evening. The moment they were both in the vehicle, Angie and Miki started yelling. That was at six. Sara looked at the clock on the nightstand. It was now ten-twenty and these bitches were still at it. Well, she really wanted to go to this thing, so she wasn't waiting a minute longer.

"She is not wearing *that*."

"And exactly what is wrong with this?" Miki demanded as she held up a long, but very pretty sundress. Where the hell Miki got that dress from, Sara had no idea. It definitely didn't come from either of their closets…and never would either.

"She's not a nun. She's a horny girl who needs to get laid. The least we can do, as her friends, is help her out. That's why she should wear this." Angelina held up the tiny, black hot pants she still had clutched in her hand. Forget the scars on her leg, Sara wouldn't wear that fucking thing on principle.

"That's just trashy," Miki snapped. "She's not going out like that. *Ever.*"

Sara was done. These idiots would go all night if she didn't do something. She pushed herself away from the wall she'd been leaning against and headed toward the door. Her friends stopped arguing as Sara walked by them. She didn't even glance in their direction.

Not willing to leave her wardrobe decisions up to these two psychos, Sara tied her hair into a loose French braid, threw on a green camouflage skirt that landed just above her knee, with a slit up the right side of her leg. Then she added her favorite old pair of black cowboy boots, her thin but deadly weapon concealed inside its leather, and a green tank top. For good measure, she even had on her black cowboy hat pulled low in front of her face.

She stormed out of her house, but not before yelling, "You two bitches coming or what?"

ᘉ ᘉ ᘉ

"*Little* party?" That was the third time Miki had said the same thing. It started an hour ago as they waited in a long line of cars heading to the park. Then they waited for a parking space. Now they were standing in a long line of people waiting to get into what Sara knew to be a huge all-night rave. A well-organized, well-run rave.

"Christ, would you quit complaining." Angelina was already grooving to the pounding music. "Just relax."

Sara shook her head. Angie could enjoy herself anywhere—even in line.

It took awhile but they finally made it to the entrance. Large hulking men took money and checked for weapons, which seemed to relax Miki—at least a bit.

Sara stood in front of them. She was hoping this thing wouldn't cost a fortune. She only had fifty dollars in her pocket.

The largest of the men looked down at Sara. He stared at her and, for a moment, she wondered if he somehow saw the blade she'd hidden in her boot. Instead he nodded. "Go on in."

Sara scratched her forehead in confusion. "I...uh..."

"What's up?" Angelina asked from behind her.

"They can go, too."

"But—"

"You're on the list."

Except he hadn't checked his list. He hadn't done anything. Just kind of looked at her.

"Sweet!" Angelina cheered. "Let's go."

Before Sara could ask any questions, Angelina shoved her past the men and into a huge clearing. In the center were a couple hundred people dancing. Booths selling food, liquor and T-shirts separated the clearing from the dense forest the three friends had hunted in more than once.

Sara had never seen anything like this before. She'd gone to quite a few raves in her less-than-wild past, but they were always near or in Austin. This was her boring hometown. Raves didn't come out this far.

Angelina stood next to her and, her beautiful face flush with excitement, raised both arms in the air and let out a "Whoooowho! This fuckin' rocks!" Grabbing Sara's arm, Angie yanked her right into the dancing, writhing crowd. Miki followed and for the first time in a long time, Sara saw her smile.

It had been a couple of years since the last rave they'd gone to together. Miki had school and two jobs. Angelina had her own business, although she never seemed to be there—"That's why I have a staff." And now that they knew there was no biker gang waiting to drug them, rape them, and send them off to Taiwan to be whores—Miki's contention—the friends silently decided that on this clear, chilly night they would relax and just have a good time.

രു രു രു

Zach easily caught the beer Conall tossed at his head without his eyes ever leaving the partying crowd.

"Crowd looks pretty good tonight, huh?" Conall walked behind Zach, his own beer grasped firmly in hand.

"Guess." Zach took a long gulp, and went back to scanning the crowd.

"Not here yet, is she?"

Zach glanced at his friend. "Who?"

Conall smirked. "Zach, don't bullshit me."

He was right, of course. Zach *was* looking for her. He couldn't stop himself from looking for her. He hadn't stopped thinking about her since she shoved her tongue in his mouth.

"Oh, her." He tried to sound disinterested. "Yates still wants me babysitting her. That's all."

"Yeah. That's all." Conall could at least *pretend* to buy his brand of bullshit.

"She's probably not coming anyway. Your big-mouthed girlfriend probably talked her out of it."

"I have to ask you not to call the woman I love my girlfriend—she's my future wife!" Zach shook his head at Conall's goofy grin. A goofy grin that successfully hid a predator. "Besides," his friend continued, "that Latina was definitely coming and I'm thinking she's not coming here without 'em."

Zach hoped Conall was right. He needed to see Sara. To prove to himself she wasn't anything but a distraction. A problem to be solved. Nothing more. *Yeah, right.*

It was the "Whoooowho! This fuckin' rocks!" that caught his and Conall's attention. Christ, these women were loud.

Zach looked through the crowd, his eyes picking up images others would never see. He caught sight of her quickly. Angelina dragging Sara and the other one to the middle of the rave. This was definitely not their first all-night rave. They had no purses. No jackets. And they were prepared to sweat the night away.

Angelina had her long hair in a ponytail, allowing the black bustier she wore to be seen in all its tight, form-fitting glory. Plus, baggy blue jeans and sneakers. And the thong peeking out from under her jeans a nice, sexy touch. The one with the mouth had on a tight belly shirt displaying a gorgeous set of abs he could hear Conall growling over, shorts, and hiking boots.

Sara sported a tank top, green camouflage skirt with cowboy boots, and a hat that on anyone else he would have said looked stupid. Yet it worked for her. Although he figured she wore it to hide the scar on her face, the logic of which completely escaped him.

Sara didn't dance. Her damaged leg prevented that. But she moved really well. Nothing elaborate or fancy, and her moves weren't exactly "stripper-hot", which he and Conall learned to appreciate over the years.

Whatever she did, though, made his dick bang against the inside of his jeans demanding release…release into her.

Tragically, Conall was not fairing so well. "My. God. She is the *worst* dancer I've ever seen."

Zach had forgotten there was anyone else at the rave until Conall spoke. He glanced over and took in Miki's idea of dancing. It was kind of sad…and frightening. Yet clearly she was having a good time.

"But," Conall added, "her ass looks great in those shorts."

Zach shook his head, the man was absolutely hopeless.

ଔ ଔ ଔ

Miki snarled and swung around again, looking behind her.

"Okay. I didn't imagine *that!*" she screamed over the pulsing music.

Sara and Angie glanced at each other and back at Miki.

"What are you talking about?" Sara asked.

"Someone keeps sniffing my ass."

After a long moment of staring at her, Sara and Angie finally burst out laughing.

"It's not funny!"

"Yes it is!" they said in unison.

Before Miki could storm off, Sara grabbed her arm and pulled her back. "Dude, it's okay. Not a big deal. They're probably rolling or something and your ass just happened to be there."

"That's no excuse to…" Miki made a strange face then leaned in and whispered in her ear, "…sniff my ass!"

"I know. It's definitely in bad taste, but I wouldn't sweat it too much. Okay?"

"I just wish I had my shotgun." Miki glared at the people around her. "Cause someone would be wearing some goddamn buckshot!"

❧ ❧ ❧

Zach motioned to two of the men in charge of security. There were others he could call on, but he trusted these two to do what he told them to.

"See that guy over there?" He pointed and both men looked at the guy who had harassed Sara in her truck the morning before. "I want him to go away and not come back."

One of the men, affectionately referred to as Ox, frowned. "You want him to go away…forever?"

Zach closed his eyes. "No." And it took all his strength not to finish with, "Dumbass."

"Just make him leave and I don't want him back tonight. But I don't want any unidentified bodies tomorrow morning."

"Got it." Ox and his partner walked off and Conall suddenly slid out of the dancing crowd and again stood beside Zach.

It was the forced innocent look on his face that had Zach shaking his head.

"You sniffed her ass, didn't you?"

Conall didn't even bother hiding his grin.

❧ ❧ ❧

After about a full hour or so of straight dancing, Miki motioned that the water bottle she'd brought with her was empty. Sara and Miki moved through the crowd, leaving Angelina behind. She'd found herself a nice group of beautiful boys to dance with and seemed happy enough.

"Great music, huh?" Miki asked when they finally extricated themselves from the dancing bodies.

"Amazing!" There were top-notch European DJs here. Sara recognized several of them from music magazines and a few high-level Austin raves. How did some, to quote Miki, "low-life bikers" get DJs like these to come out to the middle of nowhere?

The pair made their way to the edge of the park grounds. The first booth they hit manned by two tall women.

"Is it me or are a lot of these females mammoth size?" Miki muttered, almost to herself. Almost. Clearly the two women heard her as they turned and glared.

"Two waters." Sara spoke quickly hoping she could avoid one of those fights caused by Miki's big mouth.

One of the women moved over to them and looked at Sara. Looked at her hard for several long seconds. *Uh-oh, I am going to have to fight. Fuckin' Miki!* Sara clenched her hand into a tight fist, ready to use it if necessary, as she closely watched the woman reach under the fold-out table and grab two waters and hand them over.

Sara, releasing a breath, went to pull cash out of her back pocket but the woman stopped her. "Take it. No charge."

Sara looked at the sign clearly listing water bottle prices. And the tiny bottles she held were five dollars each. This was getting weird.

"Why?"

"Take the water and go." Without another word, the woman returned to her friend.

"What the hell—"

"Hi." Sara and Miki discovered Miki's big blond stalker standing next to them. He nodded at Sara but smiled at Miki.

"Hi," Sara answered. "Nice *little* party."

"Thanks. Name's Conall." It was like Sara and the other three hundred people weren't even there."

Miki blinked. "Great."

It was, in fact, physically painful to watch Miki and Conall stand there, with absolutely no idea what to say next.

"Well…" Miki glanced at Sara, and Sara let her know with one look she was on her own. Mostly because she found the whole thing funny as hell…and cute. Very cute.

Glaring at Sara, Miki decided to make a break for it. "Bye." Miki took her bottle of water and walked off.

Sara's head tilted to the side as she watched the dejected expression on Conall's face. Nope, she simply couldn't help herself. "Well, don't just stand there. Go get her."

Conall sighed. "I think she hates me."

"Are you kidding? She really likes you. She's just shy."

"Really?" With that, he disappeared into the crowd, searching for the elusive Miki.

Sara let out a laugh as she realized Miki would make her pay dearly for this tomorrow.

"Having a good time fuckin' with my friend?"

Or she may be paying for it a lot sooner.

He was behind her, his hot breath in her ear, as he leaned into her. He didn't touch her, but her entire body was on fire wanting him to touch her.

"I didn't…" She couldn't even finish her sentence. *This is getting ridiculous!* She forced her body to move away from him. "Look, I don't have to explain myself to you," she snapped and turned to face him. Great. The sleeveless Harley T-shirt he wore, revealing extremely large tanned muscular arms sporting tattoos on both triceps and his left forearm, so did not help her composure. She did always have a thing for guys with tattoos. "And I'm sure your sturdy friend there can take care of himself."

"Against *her*? Are you kidding? That girl's mean as a snake."

"No, she's—don't talk about my friends."

"Don't mess with mine."

"Fine."

"Fine."

The two stood staring at each other, and Sara didn't know whether to punch him in the stomach or lick the black tribal tattoo on his right shoulder.

In order to avoid both, she turned and walked away. She'd gotten several feet when she realized he was walking beside her. She stopped. "What?"

"I didn't say a word."

Sara took several more steps but realized he was still there with her. She stopped again, this time turning to face him. "What are you doing?"

"Living life to its fullest."

Sara's eyes narrowed. "Go away."

"Why?" Zach leaned into her, but still didn't touch her. "Do I make you nervous?"

She snorted. "Please. I've known tougher gangs than you people." She started walking again, but stopped short when she realized he was no longer walking with her. It was what she had asked for but she didn't expect him to actually listen. She looked back at him. "What?"

"Well," he stated softly as he slowly moved toward her, his muscles rippling. *Godammit!* Those rippling muscles were driving her absolutely crazy. "At first, I stopped because I didn't know why you were calling me a gang member. Then I was just watching your ass move in that skirt. That pretty much kept me rooted to the spot."

Sara rubbed her nose to hide a smile. "Sorry I insulted you. Do you prefer Motorcycle Club?"

"You do know that we're not some kind of biker gang, right?"

Of course they were. How could they not be? Groups of grown adults in black leather didn't move around in packs, living together and throwing wild raves if they weren't a gang.

"We just like to ride. We like the freedom."

"Then you guys are…"

"Business partners. We own and operate a bunch of clubs."

"Really?" Sara took a sip of her water as Zach dug into the back pocket of his jeans. She would love to dig into the back pocket of his jeans herself.

Jesus, girl! Get a grip.

"Here." He handed her a business card. It was on high-quality card stock and the letters were embossed, but all it had was his name and a cell phone number.

Sara held the card up. "And?"

"Only reputable business people have business cards."

Sara loved his sarcasm. It was so ridiculous. "And the Hells Angels have their own Web sites. They sell T-shirts." Sara started walking again. Her leg began to tighten up, but she desperately hoped she could walk the pain off. She didn't want the night to end. She was, as much as she hated to admit it, having a great time with Zach.

He was a fun idiot.

Still she had yet to figure out why this guy was spending any time with her. There were women around this place who would drop to their knees at just a wink from him. She watched them watch him. And yet he seemed to be ignoring them completely. Ignoring them for *her*. She wondered what he was up to. She looked at him out of the corner of her eye. *Dammit, what is he thinking?*

ରେ ରେ ରେ

I'd give my eye teeth to have this woman sitting on my face right now.

ରେ ରେ ରେ

"Pole."

"What?"

"You're about to walk into a…" Zach walked face first into a pole between two booths. "…pole."

Zach took a step back and grabbed his forehead. "Motherfucker!"

"Don't be a whiner." Sara turned him so he faced her, pulling his hands down from his face. "Here. Let me see." Using the tips of her fingers on his expansive shoulders, she lowered him so she could examine his head. "I don't even think you'll have a bruise."

"Will you nurse me back to health if it's a concussion?"

Sara smiled, even as her entire body tightened at his husky whisper. "No. I'll leave you alone. Naked. Food for the wolves."

"Naked, huh?"

"Therapy." She pushed him away or, at the very least, tried. "For many, like you, it's a viable option." She walked past him, hoping he didn't hear her voice catch, or see that her nipples were burrowing a hole through her tank top.

Zach was doing his best to keep some semblance of self-control around Sara. But she wasn't making it easy on him. Letting him walk into poles. Touching his shoulders. Using the word "naked".

And the woman was completely oblivious to the hold she had over him. She watched everyone but him. Constantly scanning the crowd, prepared for any sign of trouble. He realized while her friends partied and danced she watched their backs and her own.

What an amazing female. The perfect wolf. The perfect mate.

Zach slapped the back of his neck to stop the treacherous errant thought. Sara looked up, startled.

"Mosquito," he offered to her unasked question.

She blinked. "Bet he's really dead now."

"You know, we should go out some time. Like a date or something."

Sara stopped. "So, let me guess. Is this 'get the townie into bed' or do you and your buddies have a bet about who can nail the cripple?"

Zach turned and gazed at her. Simply stared. But when that big grin spread across his face, Sara didn't know whether to run or just scream for help. "You are one mean bitch."

He didn't say it with any malice. In fact, he sounded kind of...turned on. Sara took a step back. He took a step toward her. "I *do* make you nervous."

"Bullshit." Well, at least she sounded like she meant that.

Zach's hand reached for her shoulder. Sara stood her ground even though she felt like high-tailing it out of there and heading home to her nice boring house. His fingers went to the Celtic tattoo on her shoulder, tracing the design with his forefinger. She felt her throat get dry and her pussy wet.

"You know," his voice was low, like a caress across her skin, "you are an amazing piece of work."

She raised an eyebrow. "I'm a bitch. I know it and I've learned to accept that flaw in my character."

"Sounds like you embrace it."

"And if I do, what do you care?"

Zach's fingers slid past her tattoo and up to her throat. She fought the urge to flinch, thinking he was going to touch the scarred part of her face. She'd never let anyone that close to her. Not her friends. Not her ex-boyfriends—nobody. And she wasn't about to let Zach get that close either. Besides, she was feeling that desire again. That desire to lick his tattoo or punch him in the stomach.

"Nice hat, by the way," he muttered softly.

So, it was going to be the punch in the stomach. Good. That she could handle.

Then Sara dropped to one knee, the sudden flaring pain in her leg nearly blinding her. Nearly as bad as what had hit her in front of her house, she gasped for air, trying not to scream. Trying not to die merely from the pain alone.

But this was Texas. Someone must have a gun here. Surely they could shoot her in the head, put her out of her misery. She wanted to yell, "Somebody kill me!" But instead she gritted her teeth against just screaming wildly.

Then she felt strong arms wrap around her and a deep voice in her ear. "Hold on. I got ya."

"Get. Off. Me."

She heard him chuckle. "Get the fuck over it."

One minute she looked like she was about to punch him in the face—he knew that hat comment would get her—looking more and more aroused the more he touched her. Then she dropped, biting back a scream of pure pain. Before Zach knew it, he was lifting her off the ground and taking her away as quickly as possible. He saw the others watching her. Smelling her weakness. Hearing the cry of pain she was desperately—admirably—trying to stifle.

He took her away from the rave and into the woods he and Conall had just been hunting in a few hours before. They'd found a small shack that had been deserted for what looked to be decades and it would give her some time to get over the pain and get her strength back. He would be there in case she needed some medical attention or something. He was just going to be there as her babysitter. Just what Yates asked him to do. Nothing more.

Yeah, right.

Chapter Ten

Sara felt herself lowered onto something hard and sturdy. She opened her eyes, easy enough now that the pain had begun to subside, and looked around what appeared to be a less-than-pleasing shack.

At least this time I didn't pass out.

"Where the hell am I?"

Zach lit a lantern someone left behind. "Feeling better?"

Sara glanced down at the dirty, dust-covered cabinet she sat on. "Nice digs."

"Well, you know, we try." Zach stood in front of her. "So, feel better or what?"

Wow, the man simply radiated warmth and charm. "Much better thank you. I'm ready to go back."

"No," he stated simply.

Yup, she still wanted to punch him in the face.

"Does the pain get like that a lot?"

Sara shrugged casually. "No. Not really." He knew she was lying. She saw it on his handsome face. The way those hazel eyes slowly rose to meet hers. The little half-smirk on his lips and the slightly raised eyebrows.

"Look it didn't used to, but lately…" Sara had to stop because she'd begun to cry.

For months, she'd been fighting the pain and terror all on her own, not even telling Miki and Angelina. She knew her friends well enough to know they'd worry—and drive her crazy in the process. Besides, they'd insist she go into the hospital. Lynette had always warned her, "Hospitals only kill ya." And, except for the constant pain, she'd been remarkably healthy her entire life. What exactly where they going to do for her now, after all these years? So she'd decided to continue living with the pain, and had. Quite successfully, in fact. Until the last few months when everything went from bad to worse.

Sara buried her face in her hands and quietly wept for several long moments...until he touched her. Not on the shoulder or her knee. He touched her scar. Problem was she had successfully hidden it under her skirt. Her sexy slit wasn't even on that side.

With a growl, Sara's hand shot out and grabbed his wrist before it could move further up her leg. The rough tips of his fingers dragging lightly across her scar didn't hurt. It didn't hurt at all. Instead, it felt damn amazing.

"What the hell?" she barked, trying to ignore the sudden burning desire she had to get this man naked.

"I needed you to stop feeling sorry for yourself. Only thing I could think of." She tried to push his arm away, but it was like steel and it wasn't moving. Didn't help he was smiling at her either. And that he had the sweetest smile she'd ever seen. She wanted to slap that smile right off his face. *Smug prick.*

"You know, it's amazing you lasted this long. After what you've been through."

"You being a smart ass?"

"If I were being a smart ass I'd say something else about your hat."

Sara tore the hat off her head. "*Happy now?*"

"Thrilled," he muttered as he pried her hand off his arm. Once accomplished, he pushed her skirt up above her scar.

Shelly Laurenston

Working hard not to panic or fall all over the man like a slobbering puppy, she demanded, "What exactly are you doing?"

"Nothing," he lied as he ran his hand over her thigh, increasing her pleasure, although she did her best not to enjoy it. The bastard wasn't even looking at her but kept watching his own hand move over her flesh. Eventually, the other hand joined in to move along the back of her knee and the bit of exposed calf above her boot. She watched his hands too, marveling at how big they were. They had light scars, faded over time and tanned from exposure to the sun. Nails clipped or bitten down as low as possible without hitting the quick. And now those tanned, scarred hands were slipping between her thighs and slowly pulling her legs apart.

She bolted straight up, but he shook his head, still not looking at her. "Don't. You're distracting me."

Distracting him? Was he serious? *She* was distracting *him*?

His right hand moved back to massaging her scar while his left hand went deeper between her thighs. His thumb ran along the seam of her ultra-fancy Jockey For Her bikini briefs for about three seconds before he simply ripped them off. Sara gasped, her body jerking forward. And, before she could stop herself, before she could think about the logic of this one action or punching herself in the face, she slammed her lips against his. Her tongue slipped into his mouth, while his thumb slipped between the folds of her sex. She leaned into his hand and his thumb slowly circled her clit.

Moaning into his mouth, her arms went around his neck, but he pulled back .

If he stops I'm going to wring his big neck.

But he didn't stop, instead his hands went under her hips and roughly yanked her to the edge of the cabinet she was on. Crouching in front of her, he pushed his head between her legs. Grabbing the sides of the cabinet, Sara held on for dear life.

Sara knew she should stop him. Knew she should slap his face and limp off, her head held high. She should be home, safe—and alone—in bed watching another episode of "Seinfeld" for the four-thousandth time. She definitely shouldn't be here, leaning back, letting a stranger bury his head between her legs and ever so slowly swirl his tongue around her clit, taking up where his finger left off. No, she really shouldn't. But Sara didn't want to stop him. Instead, she snaked her hands through his brown hair and spread her legs farther apart. And then, to ensure her place as a slut, she arched her back and pulled his head closer into her. She felt him chuckle against her burning flesh and a low growl erupted from her throat.

Big hands gripped her thighs, holding her steady as Zach worked his tongue around and in her. No one had ever gotten her this crazy before. This hungry to be fucked. And Zach was doing it all with his tongue. Christ, what was she doing? Had she lost her mind? Maybe she finally had, but who was she kidding? Nothing in her life before had ever felt this good. Absolutely nothing. Her fears of the last few months, her pain—all forgotten as Zach's tongue fucked her.

It was the way he did it. He didn't rush it or her. He took his time, savoring the taste of her. Eating her out like she had the most important pussy on the planet.

And when he began to swipe his tongue up and down her clit, the low growl he'd steadily pumped out of her exploded into a scream as an orgasm tore from her gut and straight up her spine. She gripped his head tighter as she came and came, and his tongue kept moving and licking, bringing on wave after wave of killer pleasure.

In the same moment, she felt a sharp pain in her thigh where her scar was, but it only lasted a second and was gone. Compared to what she'd put up with the last few months, she barely noticed it.

Panting, Sara slumped back against the wall, her eyes closed, her fingers finally loosening from his thick hair. He slowly pulled away but not before he licked the inside of her thigh which, inexplicably, Sara found really sweet.

Maybe she would go to sleep right here. In this dingy little shack. But the sound of cloth ripping forced her to open her eyes. Zach had taken off his T-shirt and was tearing it into several strips. She marveled at his body. Tanned skin stretched over thick muscles as broad shoulders and chest narrowed into a tapered waist. The bastard simply had no idea how gorgeous he was, or the affect he had on her.

"Looks like I scratched your leg a bit."

She looked at her thigh but he'd already wrapped material around it. To be blunt, she really didn't give a shit. Right at the moment, she didn't give a shit about anything.

Until she heard Miki screaming her name a few hundred feet from the shack. There was no way in hell she'd explain this little scenario to her friends. Not in this lifetime. Without thinking, Sara snapped to attention, kneeing Zach right in the face. "Oh, sorry," she mumbled absently. She pushed him out of the way, slammed her hat back on her head, and charged out the door.

Zach sat on the floor of what even he would consider a hovel. His favorite T-shirt in shreds, his jaw in complete agony from where her knee slammed into it, and the taste of Sara's pussy still fresh and sweet on his tongue. And he was busy trying to figure out what the hell happened.

He had one simple mission for himself when he brought her here. To stop her pain. It was killing her. He could see that as plainly as her cute little nose. And he figured he needed to try Marrec's suggestion of bleeding her. From there he decided explaining the truth would scare her off, so he had to distract her somehow. Okay, simple enough. Since his hands on her appeared to make her quite happy, why not a hand job? Hell, it couldn't hurt. Only five minutes out of his day. At least that was the plan. But the more he rubbed her leg, the more his dick got hard. The more she made that sound in the back of her throat, the more his dick got hard. And then she kissed him. Like that first night, but she wasn't drunk. She knew exactly what she was doing and that made it even hotter. She wanted him. Before he knew it, he was practically on his knees, his face buried in her sweet little pussy. He could still feel her hands in his hair and hear that growling sound she made...

Zach gave a growl of his own and stood up. "Fuck this shit." He angrily yanked off his boots and jeans. Standing naked in the middle of the room, he shifted.

A few minutes later, a two-hundred-pound dark brown wolf silently padded out of the shack. He smelled her scent in the air and knew exactly the direction she'd gone to meet up with her friends—so he turned and trotted off the opposite way.

Chapter Eleven

She sailed through the intense question-and-answer portion of the evening—Where did you go? *Nowhere.* Did you see Zach? *Nope.* What happened to your leg? *Just a scratch.*

She flew through Miki's twenty minute analysis on the group's business. Some of the hottest clubs any of them had heard of in San Francisco, Seattle, New York, London, Milan. The list went on and on. Miki also analyzed why a bunch of so-called club owners would be in a dinky little town in Texas throwing a rave.

But it was Angelina's innocent "I had so much fun tonight" while they were driving home that Sara simply couldn't take the pressure any more.

"*I'm a whore!*" she screeched suddenly.

Miki hit the brakes of the white pickup, causing the vehicle to fishtail. It stopped in the middle of the deserted highway, across two lanes.

The three friends sat in the truck, not moving, not speaking. They stared out at the big, star-filled Texas sky.

Miki, her hands still gripping the steering wheel, glanced at Sara. "You're not wearing any underwear, are you?"

Sara let out a strangled squeal and buried her head in her hands.

Angelina and Miki burst out laughing.

"Bitches," Sara growled.

ଔ ଔ ଔ

It had been a busy night for Sara. A slammin' rave, head from a stranger, and shit from her friends. But she was sure it was the mere three hours of sleep making her unbelievably cranky. As soon as she got to work, Randy, her favorite cutie pie pit bull, had taken one look at her and run the other way. She almost took it personally but then she'd ripped poor Marrec's head off as soon as she walked into the shop. In response, he ran out and got her a large cup of coffee, like an offering to some evil bitch goddess, then scurried away to his workshop to finish off some guy's order. She didn't blame him or Randy. She was being a total bitch and she knew it.

Actually, that wasn't right. She blamed Zach.

What a stupid name—Zach. He was stupid. Stupid, big-armed, big-handed bastard. Both Miki and Angelina assured her she would never see the guy again.

"Honey, he's a biker. He got his wings and flew." That was after they arrived back at her house. During this portion of the conversation, she buried her head in the couch, her hands over her ears, but her friends weren't giving her a break.

"Would you prefer we lied to you?" Miki asked. "Tell you he's going to marry you and take you away from all this?"

"We love you too much to do that," Angelina added.

Yeah, sure. That was it.

Sara flipped through a magazine she found lying around the store. She figured it must be Angelina's since it had all the newest fashions, none of which Sara knew or cared about. She wasn't really reading anything. She wasn't even seeing the pictures. All she kept seeing were those big hands and those beautiful hazel eyes. She kept remembering how his tongue tasted and the feel of his hands on her legs…between her thighs…and that delicious little "swirly" thing he did with his tongue…

"Hi."

"Nothing!" she snapped, for no reason in particular. She saw Angelina in front of her.

"Hmm, I wonder what you've been thinking about?" her friend asked with mock innocence.

Sara sneered at her. "Why are you here?"

"I was just seeing how my best friend was doing after her recent bout with promiscuity."

"I'm tired and cranky."

"Clearly." Angelina tugged on her friend's leather jacket. "Come on. Let's get you out of here, cranky girl. I'll get you lunch or something."

Sara's eyes narrowed. "Did Marrec call you?"

Angelina turned on that dazzling smile. "Well, he's been hiding in the back now for two hours. You scared the shit out of him."

"Honestly." When did everybody turn into such pussies?

Sara slipped off the stool and grabbed her backpack. "I'm leaving," she yelled at the back door. "You can come out of hiding now."

Sara came around the corner and moved toward the front door. When she realized Angie wasn't next to her, she stopped and spun around. "Are you coming or what?"

The expression on Angie's face startled her. She was staring at Sara like she'd grown another head. "What? *What?*" Sara looked down at herself. "Is there a bug on me?" She slapped at her jeans, trying to get off a bug she didn't really see.

Angelina's eyes narrowed. "Honey—where's your limp?"

"My...what?" Sara asked, completely confused and distracted from slapping herself stupid.

"I've known you twenty years, Sara Morrighan. And since day one, I've watched you limp that wide ass around this town."

"Hey. It is *not* wide!"

"And now, today, I watched you practically skip to the front door like goddamn Pollyanna. Pain free. What the hell's going on?"

Sara looked down at her legs. She took a few steps. Nope. No limp. Because there was no pain. None. Stranger still, even on those rare occasions Sara didn't have pain, her leg was always so weak she still had the limp. Now it felt like her wounded left leg was as strong as her right. And both felt even stronger than that.

Sara bent her knee and raised her leg up. She stretched the leg out behind her and leaned forward. No pain. No weak muscles. Just fluid movement.

Sara had been so late this morning and so busy thinking about Zach, she hadn't even realized it. In fact, when she got out of bed she immediately started limping out of habit.

"I don't know. It hurt yesterday." *A lot.*

Angelina stood next to her now, concern written all over her face. She knew what her friend was thinking. Stuff like this didn't happen to people like them. Random events of good luck is what Miki always called it. In their world, people didn't win the lottery, meet the perfect man, or suddenly get better. And that meant only one thing...

"Oh, my God. I'm dying."

"*What?*" Angelina shook her head. "You're not dying, you idiot."

"Everything okay, ladies?" Marrec had reappeared and was watching them closely. Sara opened her mouth to tell him she was clearly dying because her leg suddenly felt better and people always felt better just before they died and she felt he should know since they'd always been so close, and to make sure her funeral was a tasteful affair—

"Everything's fine, Marrec. Thanks." Angelina pushed Sara out the door into the parking lot.

"Where's your truck?"

Sara pointed. "Over there."

Taking the keys sticking out of Sara's baggy khaki pants, Angie pushed her over to the vehicle. "Get in," she ordered.

Sara looked at her friend. "I don't want a big funeral, ya know. Just something simple."

"Would you get the fuck in the truck," Angie snapped.

ରେ ରେ ରେ

Zach had just gotten back from hunting, stopping briefly at the nearby lake to wash the blood off his fur and paws. He'd since shifted back to human and, leaving most of the Pack by the lake's edge, returned to the campsite to get dressed and track down Sara. He tried to convince himself it was simply to see how she was doing. To find out if opening her old wound helped her as he thought it might. But that was all just bullshit. He really wanted to see her. End of story.

He thought about her all night. Her smell, her taste, her hands in his hair. Her cries of passion and her growls of desire. He couldn't stop thinking about her no matter how hard he tried. Not that he tried all that hard.

Already in his jeans, Zach had just pulled on his T-shirt and boots when Marrec arrived. A few of his Pack were with him and as soon as he jumped out of his truck he made a direct line for Zach.

Zach stood to his full height, but didn't make any aggressive moves. Nor did he back down. He knew they were in this man's territory because of Marrec's goodwill, so he wasn't about to risk that by ripping the old bastard's throat out. At least not yet.

But before Marrec could get his hands on Zach, Yates and Conall, who had yet to venture down to the lake, stepped in front of their Pack mate. Yates, being Alpha, snarled, his canines extending.

"Back off, Marrec." They may be in Marrec's territory, but Zach knew Yates would never let the man get near one of his own Pack.

"You tell that bastard to keep his hands off her!"

Yates didn't need any clarification as he and Conall turned to look at Zach. "Tell me you didn't?" Yates demanded with a sigh.

Zach shrugged. "It depends on what your definition of 'didn't' is."

At that Marrec went for Zach again, but Conall pushed him back.

Yates glared at Zach before turning back to Marrec. "Is she yours? Did you mark her?"

"No!" Marrec seemed truly appalled. "She's like my daughter." He scowled at Zach again. "A very protected daughter," he growled out.

Yates sighed. "I understand that, but—"

Marrec cut him off, "Who's not ready to be turned yet."

Yates frowned in confusion. "Marrec, that usually takes years. No matter what Zach did or didn't do."

"Then why was she trotting around my store today like she was about to run a marathon? No pain. Just power. And guess what? Her friends noticed."

Yates sighed again, his canines smoothly disappearing back into his mouth. "Shit, Zach, what *did* you do?"

Zach wasn't ashamed of what he did, he simply didn't know Sara would react to it so strongly or so quickly. "I bled her old wound, just like you suggested."

"I didn't suggest shit to you!" Marrec glared straight at Zach. "And exactly how did you bleed her without her knowing what you were up to?"

When Zach didn't answer, Marrec again went for his throat. Yates and Conall pulled Marrec back.

Yates was clearly losing patience. "Marrec," he snapped as he pushed the man back for what seemed the hundredth time. "The bottom line is she's not yours. By blood or mark. So, I'm not exactly sure what your problem is."

"Did you ever see someone turned quickly? It's rare, but it happens." Marrec took a deep breath and once he seemed to be under some kind of control, Yates silently allowed him to walk over to Zach and face him. The two men stood toe to toe and, although he was a good five inches shorter than Zach, Marrec's power and why he was Alpha Male of his Pack was more than clear. "If something happens to her because of this," Marrec warned in a deadly low voice, "no one will be able to protect you from *me*."

The men locked eyes for a few more seconds; then, with a snarl, Marrec turned and walked away. The three men watched Marrec's truck pull out of their campsite.

Conall gave his friend a sympathetic look, and headed off to the lake to meet up with the rest of the Pack. When he was gone, Yates rubbed his tired, bloodshot eyes before turning to Zach. "Let's not bullshit around, okay, Zach?" When Zach didn't reply, Yates went on. "We both know what Casey is up to. But I know that it's time for me to step down, no matter what she thinks or wants. I'm tired. And I'm burnt out. I just want to be part of the Pack. Not worrying about who is doing what. And I want you to take over.

But if you fuck this up, and that girl goes down because of you...there's no Pack in the world that will have you."

"I don't care," Zach answered honestly. "You didn't see her in pain, Yates. She was dying." Zach paused for a moment. "And I wasn't going to let her."

Yates seemed mildly surprised. He slowly nodded in understanding. "Fine." Yates moved next to Zach so that he was right by him, his voice low. "Then you better watch her. Because if she turns as fast as I think she might, she *will* go down and she'll take this entire town with her."

Yates left Zach standing there in the middle of the campsite. And for the first time in Zach's life, his first thought wasn't about himself or the Pack. It was about someone else entirely. It was about Sara. The thought of anything happening to her caused his insides to clench up and his brain to shut down, leaving only one thought. He had to find her. He had to find Sara now.

Shit. Dick went hard. He would really have to do something about that.

Chapter Twelve

Sara paced back and forth inside Miki's tiny apartment. She was anxious, tense and extremely horny. This seemed odd, considering her current situation.

As soon as they left Marrec's shop, Angelina dragged her to Miki's. After banging on the door for several minutes, a clearly just-awakened Miki answered, snatching the door open. "What?"

Angelina blinked in surprise. "My God, were you actually asleep?"

"Yeah," she replied sarcastically. "I was actually asleep."

"Well, isn't that rare," Angelina stated honestly as she pushed her way past Miki, dragging Sara behind her. "You're not going to believe this shit," she announced. And before Sara knew it they'd forced her to act like a runway model, parading back and forth in Miki's tiny, book-filled living room to demonstrate how her limp had all but disappeared.

By this point, Miki was fully awake. "Honey, exactly what did that guy do to you?"

"I'm not answering that question again." Sara had given them the barest of details on her sexual exploits the night before. So she wasn't about to go into how she'd screamed and writhed under the man's tongue like a horny dog.

"Would you focus," Miki snapped. "There has to be a reason you're suddenly...okay."

Sara stopped modeling and faced her friends. "But I'm not okay. I'm dying."

"*What?*"

Angie quickly cut off the potential insanity. "You are not dying, you idiot." Staring at her friend from the safety of Miki's old couch, Angelina looked Sara up and down. "In fact, you look as healthy as a fucking horse."

"Which brings us back to the point," Miki dived in again. "What did he do to you?"

"I don't know. Nothing?"

As if rehearsed, both Angelina and Miki raised one eyebrow each, staring at their in-denial friend.

Sara sighed and crossed her arms in front of her chest, hoping to hide her hardening nipples. *Christ, just the thought of him!* "Look, I'm not telling you about...you know."

Miki rolled her big brown eyes. "I don't want to know where his tongue was—"

"Dude!"

Miki barreled on, "But did he give you anything? Any pills? Anything to drink? I mean, fuck, Sara, it *was* a rave."

Sara thought back to that night. She remembered him rubbing her thigh, kissing her thigh, licking her...*shit.*

Sara turned and charged into the bathroom, Miki and Angelina close behind. As they walked in, Sara already had her khakis down around her ankles and was turning to the mirror to examine the wound she had cleaned off and slapped a large bandage on just that morning. With one move she tore the bandage off, revealing her old scar, ripped through with four new ragged lines.

"Holy shit," Angie gasped as Miki knelt by Sara and examined her thigh. After several moments her eyes locked with Sara's.

Miki shrugged. "They look like animal marks."

"Bullshit!" Sara barked. "How would you know that anyway?"

Miki rolled her eyes. "Hello. I read *everything*."

She left the bathroom, and Sara could hear her rummaging around her apartment, pawing through the huge number of books. After a few minutes, Miki returned with a huge, dusty tome. "Here."

Grabbing the book, Sara and Angelina examined page two-hundred-and-thirty-four of the *Encyclopedia of Mammals* and saw a huge paw print. "Front paw print of six-year-old gray wolf, actual size," read the caption.

"You see?" Miki demanded.

"See what?" Sara demanded back.

"It can't be," Angelina muttered, still staring at the book.

"Exactly." Sara momentarily felt vindicated.

"The paw mark on her leg is much bigger."

"It is not a paw mark!" Sara raged as she reached down to pull her pants back up. "You are both insane!" She pushed past her friends. "I'm outta here."

Sara headed for the door, but both Miki and Angelina grabbed her just as she stepped outside.

"Oh, no you don't, missy." Angelina pulled her back in while Miki slammed the door. "Until we know what's going on, you're not going anywhere."

That had been four hours ago. Her friends still had no answers, although a lot of ridiculous theories were running rampant. So, Sara paced and paced and paced. The walls were closing in on her—at least that was how it felt. Like she was trapped. The tiny apartment caging her in. She had all this sudden, untapped energy. She wanted to go for a run or something. She needed some fresh air. What could be the harm in that?

With Angelina and Miki arguing in the bedroom in whispers, a few minutes on the porch wouldn't hurt anybody.

Moving silently to the door, Sara eased it open and slipped out into the night.

ભ ભ ભ

Zach walked into the diner, ignoring the fact all activity stopped as soon as they saw him. They were all shifters. Marrec's Pack. And word about him and Sara had moved through the small town like wildfire. He was getting exceptionally shitty treatment all over the goddamn place. They acted like he'd tried to hurt Sara.

Shit, maybe his Pack should have just grabbed the woman and run. Cause there was nothing like redneck shifters to annoy a man.

Zach leaned up against the counter and motioned to the waitress.

She stood in front of him with a less than friendly expression on her face. "Yeah?"

"Have you seen Sara?"

"Yeah," the woman replied.

Zach waited for her to finish, but she kept staring at him instead.

"Could you tell me where I can find her?" he finally asked, working really hard not to start tearing throats from bodies.

"I could tell you…"

"Okay."

"…but I won't."

CR CR CR

She knew something was seriously different as soon as she walked into Skelly's. Since the day Sara had fake I.D. she'd been coming and going out of Skelly's virtually unnoticed unless someone accidentally ran into her or a person new to Skelly's happened to spot the scar on her face.

But as soon as she walked into the club this night, she realized she had every guys' attention. True, a little overwhelming, especially at first when she didn't really know what they were looking at or why. Yet, at the same time, strangely exhilarating.

Moving through the crowd, Sara's eyes kept scanning left to right, her entire body ready to deal with whatever came at her. Actually, she kind of looked forward to something coming at her. Her senses felt on overload. Smells she'd never noticed before assaulted her, like Leon the bouncer's overuse of Old Spice. And even that couldn't block out the fact the man probably hadn't showered since the night before.

Sounds, too, seemed more intense. Louder. And the bass from the music pounding through the speaker system pulsated through her body. The feel of it almost sexual, causing her nipples to tighten and her pussy to clench. But even with the music going full blast, she couldn't understand why everyone was suddenly screaming. She could hear them fine, couldn't the person in front of them?

Sara walked up to the bar and motioned to the bartender who worked on Miki's nights off.

"Hey, Sara. Miki's not here tonight."

"Yeah. I know. Can I get a shot of..." She stopped. Mhhhm. Perhaps tequila was not the best thing tonight. "Make that a beer. Dark."

He nodded and had it in front of her in less than a minute. Before she could dig the fiver out of her pocket, a male arm reached around her. "I got it."

Sara looked over her shoulder and blinked. Kent Ethos? He didn't belong to any particular club but was definitely a rider and gave Marrec a lot of business.

"Uh…thanks, Kent."

He smiled down at her and she realized there was real intent behind that smile. "My pleasure, Sara." He leaned against the bar, staring at her like he had his eyes on the hottest piece of ass ever.

"So, you just hanging out tonight?"

Sara bit back her typically sarcastic remark and instead said, "Yeah. I guess."

"Hey, Sara."

Sara looked at the man standing on the opposite side of her. She knew him as Jazz and that was about it. And definitely part of a club. One of the tougher ones. Last she heard they still hated her by association. They never forgave Angie for what she did to their leader all those years ago. For a while Sara thought for sure they'd try and retaliate but Marrec handled it and since then they all stayed out of each other's way.

Until tonight it seemed.

"Hi, Jazz."

"So, you just hangin' out tonight?"

Sara had a hard time maintaining a neutral look on her face. She really wanted to stare at them all in shock or laugh hysterically until she peed in her pants. Especially when one of the riders from another cycle club walked up behind her and simply stood there watching her.

"Yeah. I'm just hangin'," she said somehow without laughing.

"Everything all right, Sara?"

One of Marrec's older sons stared at her from across the bar, a deep scowl on his rugged face, several of his siblings and cousins standing behind him. Uh-oh. She knew that expression. The same one they all got when they thought someone was putting Sara down or hurting her feelings.

"Yeah, she's all right," Jazz snapped. "So back the fuck off."

Uh-oh.

ରେ ରେ ରେ

Zach was about to howl in frustration when he got the call. For hours he searched for her. He eventually found out she'd gone off with her friends, but he lost her scent once she left Marrec's. Including the diner, he also tried her house, the other two restaurants in town and the local movie theater.

Then Conall called. "You better get over here."

It turned out "here" was the club he first saw her in. He had gone there earlier, but it was a quiet evening with just a few patrons hanging out so he quickly left.

But when he rode his bike up, Conall was standing outside with Kelly and Julie. Standing with them was a small group of patrons, wearing their requisite Goth black and leather. They all looked like they were waiting for something, but he was afraid to ask what.

He got off his bike and walked up to Conall. "Well? Where is she?"

"In there." Conall motioned to the club. "But you better hurry up. The owner's about to call the cops. I'll hold him off as long as I can."

Heading toward the entrance, he heard Conall's voice behind him. "Be careful, Zach."

Zach walked into the club and right into a bar fight. Several men already knocked out and bloody on the floor. But at least six other men still fighting.

He looked for Sara, assuming she'd be in the middle of it since the girl could instigate a riot among nuns. She wasn't.

In seconds, though, he picked up her scent. How he hadn't caught it five miles back, he'd never know—it was that strong and probably every male in the place responded to it.

Zach quickly located her across the room, calmly sitting on the stool watching the men fight. It hit Zach like a thunderbolt. They weren't fighting her. They were fighting *over* her. And even more annoying—she was letting them! She seemed to be thoroughly enjoying herself.

The men fighting were bikers. Gang members she'd probably known over the years who never paid much attention to her. Until now.

Okay. This is bad. But it could be worse.

Sara's gaze lifted from the men fighting in front of her. She cast around and he realized she'd picked up his scent. She turned and looked right at him and Zach felt his heart stop. The woman had been beautiful before but now…

Sliding off the stool she'd been perched on, Sara walked toward him, expertly avoiding the tangle of bloody men.

As she came close to him, she licked her lips and Zach wasn't sure how much more he could take before he lost the control he was barely holding on to.

Sara stood in front of him, a smile sliding across her full lips. She reached up and kissed him. Nothing fancy. Just her lips touching his. Then she abruptly pulled away from him.

"Have fun," she spat.

As she moved away, Zach was hit from every side by six bikers who hated his guts.

Okay. That was really *bitchy*, Sara thought as she watched Zach hit the floor. Every man she'd touched or spoken to that evening had somehow ended up in this huge brawl in the middle of her favorite club. And she knew kissing Zach would send the remainder of those idiots his way. Yet she felt he kind of deserved it.

Christ, what was wrong with her? When did she get so…bloodthirsty?

Not only that, but she never thought anyone would fight over *her*. Especially, not-even-that-drunk biker guys who'd always ignored her before. Thankfully, Marrec's sons and nephews didn't even have a chance to get involved before the bikers went after each other. Instead they stood behind her and watched the fight while protecting her at the same time.

Then she saw Zach. No, that's wrong. She didn't see him, at first. She *sensed* him, and then she smelled him. And he smelled primal and oh, so wonderfully male. Her mouth actually watered.

She debated whether to ignore him but, she thought, W*hy shouldn't the fucker fight for me, too?"* And that's where the kiss came in. She knew she had him as soon as she licked her lips. Surprisingly, Marrec's kin looked impressed when she walked back over to take her seat.

Now, however, she was starting to worry. Zach wasn't coming up out of the throng of men. And she had no intention of going home with anyone else tonight.

She was about to start dragging men off him herself, until she heard an angry snarl and saw a biker named Ray fly by. Then another and another.

In less than three minutes, Zach wiped the floor with the biggest, toughest bikers she'd ever known. Men who had done seriously hard time.

When finished, he turned and faced her. He was breathing hard, his face battered and bloody, already swelling in some spots, his lip split and dripping blood. She had the overwhelming desire to lick that blood away.

Looking at his handsome face, she had the intense feeling he was about to take her right there on the dance floor. Fuck her brains out in front of everybody. Not that she'd complain.

Zach didn't know whether to fuck her or soak her head in the toilet. Both seemed like reasonable reactions to what she pulled.

He looked at Marrec's Pack standing behind Sara, and he knew they would no longer step in to protect her crazy ass. At least, not protect her from him. He'd won her fair and square. He could drag Sara off by the hair and they wouldn't get in his way. Of course, he risked her ripping his throat out in the process and Marrec's Pack wouldn't stop that either.

He also knew his own Pack stood behind him now, watching them both. He could smell them.

"Well, well. What a mess, huh, Zach?"

He gritted his teeth at Casey's smug voice. Maybe he would fuck Sara and put Casey's head in the toilet.

Casey leaned against the bar and stared at Sara.

"How ya doin', honey? You doin' okay?"

Sara didn't answer her. Instead she stared. At first Casey was smiling, but when Sara didn't turn away, Casey lost that smile. Zach knew Casey wanted Sara to look away. Needed her to.

Without turning from her, Casey spoke to Zach. "You better put a leash on your girl there, Zach. I'd hate to have to break her in so soon."

He'd kill Casey first before he let the bitch touch Sara. "Breaking her in" being the euphemism they all used for grabbing a Beta around the throat and bringing them down until they showed their belly and learned their place. But apparently Sara wasn't about to be anybody's bitch. He caught the woman in mid-flight as she dove over the bar; her hands outstretched and reaching for Casey's throat.

Sara didn't like the way Casey was looking at her. Like she was challenging her or something. And she was standing a little too close to Zach in Sara's opinion. In fact, the bitch was just pissing Sara off. She wanted to hurt Casey. She wanted to see the bitch bleed.

So what's stopping you? Her last thought before she went for her.

But Zach stopped her, his big hands grabbing her around the waist. "Sonofabitch!"

Casey didn't move, but she was clearly rattled. Her eyes wide as she watched Sara. And apparently Sara was enough of a threat that Yates stepped between them.

Zach luckily had a good grip on her, because Sara was losing it. That's when he knew—she'd gone feral.

"You fucking whore! *Break me in? Fuck you!*"

Zach pulled her back, wrapping his arms around her body. She was shaking, but it wasn't from fear. "Easy," he whispered in her ear. "Easy."

His voice seemed to soothe her. He thought he might be able to get Sara out of there without any more problems. But not wanting to show weakness to her females, Casey continued to stare at her.

Sara pulled away from Zach and went for Casey again. He caught her on the bar and dragged her back, tossing the woman over his shoulder and heading to the exit. Sara was still screaming and banging her fists against his back demanding to be let go so she could "...*finish the little bitch!*"

He motioned to Conall who tossed the truck keys to him. He caught them in mid-air, went outside to the truck, threw Sara in, got in after her, and tore out of the parking lot.

Sara wasn't exactly sure when she turned feral, but she was curious to see where this would lead. She'd never actually "lost it" before. Miki lost it all the time. She popped off continually, like a little firecracker. Angelina seemed the most rational of the three, but everyone in town knew she had a temper that had caused some men to actually move out of Texas. No, it was a well-known fact Sara was the rational one. The one people came to for sage-like advice. The one people knew they could rely on since Miki might forget and Angie simply wouldn't care. She was Golden Retriever Sara.

Until tonight. Tonight she was Drunk-Sara without the liquor. And she finally had to admit, Drunk-Sara was fucking scary.

When the pickup truck pulled up to her house, Sara was immediately disappointed. She wanted to hit another club. Maybe go to Austin and scare some city-folk. She sure as hell didn't want to slip into her comfy clothes and watch TV for the rest of the night.

Now, if Zach wanted to keep her busy for a few hours…well that was completely different. But by the look on his face when he stopped the truck, his staying might be a remote possibility.

Sighing, she waited to see his next move.

Chapter Thirteen

Zach turned off the motor and pulled the keys out of the ignition. Clearly the woman wanted him dead. She'd thrown him under the proverbial bus, and she knew it, too.

Now what to do? Simple. Dump her ass and go. If he fucked her tonight, he was going to keep her. He knew that as surely as he knew she was crazy. And he didn't want a mate. He especially didn't want *her* as a mate. His whole life spent trying to keep her pretty ass out of trouble. He had much bigger plans than that.

Pushing open the truck door, he stepped out. Reaching back in, he dragged her across the seat, ignoring her plaintive, "Hey!"

He pulled her to him and tossed Sara over his shoulder again, walking up the porch steps to her house. The temptation to drop her on her head almost overwhelmed him, but instead he carefully lowered her to the ground. "Keys," he ordered. She took them out of her pants pocket and handed them over. He unlocked her front door and pushed her inside, following behind her.

While she stood in the middle of her living room, he double-checked the house to make sure they were the only ones there. He wasn't worried anyone might really be there; he would have smelled any Pride members before he even walked in. But doing that kept him from thinking about how good she smelled or how hot she looked in those khaki pants that were a little too big for her. They kept slipping off her waist and she kept hiking them back up.

"Everything looks safe."

"Why wouldn't it be?"

No, probably not a good time to tell her there was a whole Pride that wanted to see her dead. The mood she was in right now, she'd go looking for them.

"Never hurts to check." He headed toward the door, making sure not to touch her as he left.

"You want a drink or something before you go? I think I have tequila around here somewhere." Kicking off her sneakers, she disappeared into her kitchen.

Zach slammed the door and quickly followed. "*No!*"

Sara turned around startled.

"And you don't want any either." The last thing the woman needed was tequila.

"I don't?"

"No. No drinking. And don't go anywhere tonight. Just stay here. Be quiet. Watch TV or something."

"I see." Sara, using only her legs, hopped up on to the counter.

Zach was amazed how fast she was changing. Every second she seemed to be getting stronger. It wasn't supposed to work like this. It wasn't supposed to happen this fast. But Sara kept surprising him.

She sighed. "You don't want me to drink. You don't want me to go out. You just want me to sit here quietly. Like a good little girl."

Zach swallowed. "Right."

"Interesting." Sara leaned back, her palms resting on the countertop behind her. Her back slightly arched, her breasts pushing against her white T-shirt. She kicked her legs out, the heels of her feet banging against the wood cupboard. "You know, my friends think you did something to me."

"I *did* do something to you."

She actually blushed at that. "Something other than that. Something bad."

"What do you think?"

"Me? Oh, I think I'm dying."

Absolutely psychotic. "You're not dying." Zach couldn't help but laugh. "Why would you even think that?"

"My mother died when I was a baby. My father died in an actual *animal attack* when I was eight. My grandmother was a very unpleasant woman. And I've been limping around this town for the last twenty years. Do you really think I believe in good fortune?"

She did have a point. "But how do you feel? Do you feel like you're dying?"

She was quiet for several moments, and when she spoke her voice was low. "No. I feel strong. Powerful. I feel amazing."

"You are amazing." Okay. Where did that come from? How did those words just leave his mouth? And she seemed as surprised as he felt.

"Why, thank you tall, dark stranger."

"You forgot handsome."

"No I didn't."

Staring into those beautiful brown eyes, Zach realized he could see his future in those eyes. Everything he'd ever wanted to be or wanted to have were in those eyes.

I gotta get outta here. "I better go."

"That's not fair."

Uh-oh. "What's not fair?"

"I'm bored. I'm anxious. And you say I can't leave and I can't drink." She smiled at him. "So I'm thinking you better come up with a way to keep me occupied or who knows what kind of shit I'll get in to."

Zach had no response for that, although his dick certainly did. But he ignored it. "I better go." *That was feeble,* he thought desperately.

"Then go." She didn't sound hurt or disappointed. In fact, she sounded rather smug.

Zach got as far as the kitchen door that led into the dining room.

He turned and looked at her. "If I go, you're out the door, aren't you?"

"Well, you're not giving me a reason to stay, now are you?"

He growled. He couldn't help himself. This woman was bringing out every base instinct he had. And she knew it, too. When he growled; she grinned. She was playing with him. Playing with the beast and on some subconscious level, she knew it.

So maybe it was time to show her this was not a game she was ready for. Maybe it was time to show her what it meant to touch the beast within.

ঙ ঙ ঙ

One minute he was standing across the room. The next he was standing in front of her. Grabbing her legs, he yanked her forward, and she slammed into that brick wall he called a chest.

Sara wrapped her legs around his waist and her arms around his neck, the only move preventing her from hitting the floor.

Her breath came out in shallow gasps, like she ran up several flights of stairs. And everywhere her bare skin touched his, she felt her flesh burn. She'd never wanted anyone or anything as much as she wanted this man at this moment. Clearly she'd found an edge and she was about to go over it.

His hand reached into her hair and grabbed a handful. "You have no idea what you're doing," he growled at her. And it *was* a growl—like an angry pit bull. "I'm not nice."

Yup. There's the edge. And this is me leaping off it. "If I wanted nice," she growled back, her hand reaching into his hair and snatching his head back, "I'd fucking ask for it."

Then his mouth was on hers in a crushing, bruising kiss that left her breathless and fearing he might crack her front teeth. Laughing at the thought, she gripped Zach tighter when her body suddenly started moving. His tongue slid around hers while he carried her through the house, releasing her once they were in the bedroom.

Slowly, Zach let her slide down his long body until her feet hit the floor. He kissed her again, stopping only long enough to pull her T-shirt over her head.

The bra went with a tear, his mouth grasping one nipple as he pushed her pants over her hips so they puddled at her feet. She knew after her bra, her panties didn't stand a chance. *Yup. There they go.* He ran his hands down her back and across her now-naked ass as his mouth moved to her other nipple. Sara let out a small gasp as his teeth slid across her sensitive flesh and his hand slid between her thighs. But when his fingers stopped short of touching her pussy, she slapped his shoulder in frustration. Zach laughed and stood to his full height, looking down at her, his hand gripping one of her nipples and squeezing. "Thought I told you I wasn't nice?"

"Asshole," she ground out as the sensation of his tightening grip on her nipple went straight to her clit and stayed there.

"Bitch all you want, but you made it pretty clear…you like that I'm not nice."

Sara stared up at him. He didn't really think she'd actually respond to that statement, did he? Not when she did like the fact he wasn't some sweet teddy bear guy. True, she had no use for assholes who made her want to stab them in their sleep, but she did like her men edgy. She always had. There was something about a guy who didn't get scared about her habit of biting during sex that simply turned her on.

Zach chuckled. "You're staring at me."

"So? Are you suddenly shy?"

He grinned at that and her knees almost buckled. *Christ, what a smile.*

Sliding his hands up her body, his fingers gliding across her breasts, brushing her nipples. "Yeah. I'm very shy. Can't ya tell?" Then his hands were at her neck, holding her steady as his lips took hers. Oh, man…no one had ever kissed her like this. This man's tongue *owned* her. And he knew it, too.

While still kissing her, Zach moved her back until she felt the wall against her shoulder blades. He continued kissing her, possessing her, making sure no one else would ever be good enough for her again. Really, who the hell could live up to this? And this was just a kiss.

Sara wrapped her left leg around his waist, enjoying the fact she actually could without pain. Then any thoughts of pain disappeared as Zach thrust his jean-clad hips into her. Sara moaned at the contact. It wasn't lost on her she stood completely naked and Zach fully clothed. Actually, she found herself thoroughly enjoying it. He still wore his leather jacket and she loved the sounds it made as he moved against her. Add in that his T-shirt kept rubbing against her hard nipples while his jacket kept rubbing against her bare arms and chest and her whole body had become one throbbing, sensitive mess.

Sara knew the only one who could make it right was "big-armed, big-handed bastard" Zach.

Without warning, Zach pulled away from her but only so he could turn her around and push her back up against the wall, her palms slapping against the cold surface. He leaned into her, his body pushing against her, then he thrust his hips real slow, but this time against her ass—*oh, yeah…that works*. His erection felt like hard steel through his jeans and she had no doubt it would feel unbelievably good inside her. But he wanted to make her wait, taking his time. She admired his control and hated him for it.

His tongue connected to the flesh at the back of her neck and Sara closed her eyes, leaning her forehead against the wall. As his tongue trailed down her spine, his hands slid around and gripped her breasts. His tongue reached the cleft of her butt and went back up the way it came. He kept going until he reached her ear.

"Give me your hand," he whispered, sending a deep shudder through her entire body.

He placed his hand on top of hers and brought it down to her waist, slipping both between her thighs. Her body gave another, more violent shudder as he led the tips of her fingers to her clit and used them to slowly stroke her. A harsh breath burst from her lungs as her whole body tightened up and an intense heat began to spread from her lower back and up her spine. He growled against her flesh as he nudged her hair off to the side with the tip of his nose and began to gently nip the back of her neck. *Oh, God! Biting!* She loved biting. Not too hard and definitely not too soft—just enough pressure to make her wince and groan at the same time while not causing any unnecessary screaming or dialing of nine-one-one.

Her knees gave out and she would have hit the ground if Zach's other arm wasn't around her waist holding her in place. Her fingers, led by his, continued to firmly circle around her clit until her head fell back against his shoulder and a brutal spasm rippled through her. Gently pulling her hand away, he brought it up so they could both see it. Sara watched as he, still holding her hand wet with her own juices, slipped her middle finger into his mouth. He swirled his tongue around it and Sara used her free hand to push herself away from the wall. She turned in his arms and looked at him, her finger in his mouth.

"Clothes. Off. Now." Zach was fully dressed and she wasn't having it. She wanted him naked and inside her. Now.

Zach pulled her finger out of his mouth with a loud, wet "pop". Then she was pushing his leather biker jacket off his shoulders, letting it drop to the floor before snatching the black T-shirt off his body. She unzipped his jeans and shoved his hard body back on the bed. Raised up on his elbows, Zach watched her with a smile while she yanked off his boots and pulled off his jeans. She chuckled over his boxers and then dragged them off his body, leaving scratches along his thighs. She stood back and stared at his erection. Just stared at it. He wasn't sure exactly what she might be thinking until she looked up at him, and smiled. "Rock on."

Laughing, he wondered how in hell he ended up with this crazy bitch. Well, this hot crazy bitch.

"Wait." She ran out of the room, leaving Zach and his desperate erection lying there.

He could hear her tearing through the living room of her house, muttering "Where is it? Where the fuck is it?" to herself.

"Get your tight ass back in here," he ordered.

"Keep your balls in check. I'm coming."

"You will be if you get your ass back in here."

"Here." Sara tossed a brown paper bag on the bed beside Zach as she moved purposely into the room.

The bag landed and it popped open, boxes of condoms falling out over the bedspread. Zach smiled triumphantly. "I knew that's what you had in that bag!" He laughed until Sara dropped to her knees at the foot of the bed.

Zach's smile faded and a low groan escaped his lips. She ran her tongue along the underside of his dick, the tip gliding along the thick veins. She reached the head and swirled her tongue around it like he had her finger. Slowly she took him in her mouth and he dropped back against the bed, fighting for control. He wasn't going to take her. He'd fuck her, but he wasn't going to take her. No matter what she did to him or his dick.

He kept repeating that thought to himself over and over again, like a mantra.

Sara really had no idea what she was doing to him, though. If she had she wouldn't have deep-throated him, her left hand wrapped around the base of his dick, until he could feel the back of her throat with the tip. Then the bitch growled—*Fuck! Not the growl!*—and he felt the sensation all the way up the shaft to his balls, which she'd firmly gripped in her right hand.

She rode him with her mouth, the sound of her sucking and growling and his moaning the only thing heard in the room. And that's when he decided—she was his. He was going to claim her and claim her now.

He grabbed her by the hair, roughly pulling her off his dick. She looked at him, surprised but definitely curious. Taking her by the shoulders, he threw her onto the bed, slipping the condom on the last rational thought he had as he sat up and flipped her on her stomach. Zach knelt behind her and, gripping her by the waist, yanked her back until she was against his dick. He didn't waste any time with coaxing words or sweet endearments. She was wet and he was ready. He slammed into her and let her throaty scream wash over him, making him harder and more desperate to bury himself inside her.

Growling, he slammed back into her with such force she let out a gasp that sounded suspiciously like "Fuck!" So he slammed into her again. Leaning forward, he kissed her back as he mercilessly pounded into her. He found a muscled spot below her right shoulder, kissing and licking it as his hand reached around and found her slippery wet pussy. He clamped onto her clit as he bit down onto her back, his canines extending to tear into the flesh.

An animalistic scream ripped out of Sara's throat, her hips continuing to pump back to meet his thrusts. He felt the walls of her pussy tighten around him and he knew she was coming. Knew she was his. He held on to her shoulder with his teeth as his tongue licked at the blood and his fingers worked her clit. He slammed into her hard again. And again. That's when she screamed out his name and he felt her juices flow over him and down her thighs, her body shaking as the orgasm spread through her. Releasing her, his teeth slid out of her skin. Then he couldn't hold back anymore and with a roar he came inside her.

When the last shudder passed through them both, they collapsed on the bed and the only thought Zach had before falling into an exhaustive sleep was simple.

Goddammit.

Chapter Fourteen

Zach heard her growls and forced himself awake. Still dark out, he knew it was very early morning.

He looked down at Sara. Still sleeping, her body racked with tremors as things inside her moved and settled. Her body adjusting to its new state. Changing. Adapting. Becoming like him.

Wrapping his arms around her to keep her from hurting himself, he realized too late he should have been more worried about himself when it came to his little psychopath.

She loosened one arm from his grip and her claws barely missed slashing his throat out. Asleep but fighting him, Sara went for him again. Zach grabbed both her wrists and pushed her arms over her head. Waking her up wouldn't do any good. Not when she was like this.

One of the problems with turning shifters so late was what their bodies went through. These kind of changes should have taken place when she was in her adolescence. Then her parents would have taught her all she needed to know, helping her to adapt to being something more.

Nothing he could do about that now except deal with her slow evolution.

Although, her already having claws was a little surprising but probably not something she'd be able to control for quite a few years.

Yawning and holding her in place, Zach waited while her body calmed down and her growling subsided. He'd almost slipped back asleep, her comfortably nestled in the circle of his arms, when a sudden surge of strength hit her and she flipped him onto his back.

Uh-oh.

"Sara."

But she couldn't hear him. Her eyes still closed, she leaned down and sniffed him, then groaned. She nuzzled him under the chin and her lips barely touched his as she swiped them across.

He still had her wrists in his hands but he'd really have to slam her down to get her under control. She-wolves were incredibly strong and the perfect bedmates for the males. But with her body changing, it could get...intense.

Of course, that's when his dick sat up and said, "Oh, yeah! Go for it!"

No, no. Sara was nowhere ready for how rough the party could get between mates. Christ, how many times had the sounds of his parent's antics behind their bedroom door shocked him and his sister out of their teen minds? Their matings always sounded closer to mutual assault then any human's idea of "making love". Still, the next morning, while he and his sister scarfed down their waffles and bacon, his parents nuzzled and kissed like new lovers.

Not all, but most wolves liked it rough. Zach definitely liked it that way, but he didn't want to hurt Sara. She couldn't handle any of this yet.

So, trying for that whole gallant thing he'd never really been good at, Zach's hold on Sara's wrists tightened.

"Sara. Wake up."

Those astounding brown eyes popped open but he'd bet hard cold cash she was only half awake. And, goddamnit, she was feral. Again.

She ground her hips against his, her sex wet and hot against his stomach. "Fuck me, you shit," she growled out.

Okay!

No!

Zach gritted his teeth, fighting himself and this crazy woman at the same time. "Sara. You need to calm down." She *needed* a horse tranquilizer.

Sara fought his hold on her wrists and it was a struggle. Her strength growing every second he was around her.

"Fuck me or I'll find someone who will."

Raising one eyebrow, Zach now fought hard not to laugh. "Really?" he couldn't help but ask.

Even feral, her adorable face screwed up into a frown. "No. It has to be you. I want you." Through clenched teeth, she snapped, "So fuck me already!"

"Sara..."

But she couldn't hear him, not with that new tremor coursing through her body. Her head flung back, her long hair brushing against his thighs, she writhed on top of him.

He clenched his jaw, holding her tight and watching her. God, he'd never wanted anyone as much as he wanted her. Still, he couldn't...right?

After a few more moments, she looked back down, the aftershocks still causing her to shake. Her eyes opened and for less than a second he watched them shift to wolf and back to human.

Panting hard, she begged, "Please, Zach. God, please fuck me."

Zach nodded, unable to deny her anything at this point. And unable to deny himself—or his dick—either.

Holding onto her wrists, he sat up, pushing her back in the process. Once up, he shoved her back into the mattress. She started to sit up.

"Don't," he snarled, "even think about moving."

She lay back, staring up at him with those feral eyes.

Reaching over, he grabbed one of the unopened condom packets scattered across the bed. "You trust me, beautiful?"

She watched him, one second staring at his hands while they slipped the condom on his raging hard dick, next staring into his eyes. "No," she finally answered. "I don't trust anybody but my friends."

"Do you like me?"

"Not particularly."

"Good." He stepped off the bed, grabbed her ankles and swung her around while yanking her down so her ass rested at the very edge. "That makes this so much more fun."

The animal inside her snapped and she kicked out her foot, trying to hit him in the nuts. She'd gotten fast, but not fast enough. He slapped her foot out of the way, then placed his arms under her knees, pulling her wide open. Her pussy glistened and he could easily see the wetness on the inside of her thighs.

She struggled to get her legs free, so she could probably kick the shit out of him. She wanted to control this and probably thought she had.

Now he'd gone and pissed her off. *Good.*

Zach lifted her ass up, placing his cock right against her pussy. "Look at me, Sara."

Those intense—and currently feral—brown eyes focused on him. Nope. No logic or reasonable thought there. She'd lost those for the moment, it seemed.

Instead of bothering with trying to calm her down or prepare her, Zach slammed his cock into her instead.

Sara let out a scream, her back arching off the bed. He held her legs in his arms while he pumped his dick inside her.

Hands twisting in the sheets, her body writhing under his forceful fucking, Sara whimpered. Sweat broke out over both their bodies and Zach fucked her harder.

"Play with your tits, Sara," he ordered her. She glared at him, her lips pulling back over bright white canines. "Do it," he pushed, flashing his own fangs.

Snarling like an annoyed pup, Sara gripped her breasts in both hands and squeezed. Her snarl turned into another whimper and her pussy tightened around his dick, showing them both how much she was loving it. "Tug on your nipples with your fingers. Get 'em hard for me, beautiful."

She did, her face softening as her fingers played with her breasts.

"Oh, yeah," he moaned. "Just like that."

She grinned and it felt like his dick doubled in size. How could one woman's smile make him so hard?

"Does that feel good?" he asked, working hard to control his own impulse to come all over her.

"Yeah," she moaned out.

"Do it a little harder. Imagine it's my mouth sucking on you."

Sara wiggled a bit as she twisted her nipples and her pussy slammed down on him like a vise.

"Yeah. That's it, beautiful."

He shuddered and fucked her harder, longer. Unable to stop.

"Please, Zach."

"Please what, Sara? Tell me what you want, beautiful."

Hands still gripped her breasts, played with her nipples while sweat poured off her, leaving the bedding beneath her soaked.

"I need to come." She writhed desperately and he knew with the right touch she'd go off like an underground volcano reaching topside.

"You sure you're ready? Sure you want it bad enough?" he spit out between gasps for air.

Like that she went feral again, that snarl roaring right back. "Just do it!" She leaned up, brown eyes ripping through him. Her voice more wolf than human. "Make me come or I'll tear your throat out!"

Christ, what a vicious little bitch. And defnitely what he'd always wanted. He couldn't get deep enough inside her. Couldn't get close enough to her. He wanted to crawl inside her and stay there forever.

Zach pushed her farther back on the bed while bringing his knees up on the mattress. He left her legs resting across his thighs, leaning down to look her right in the face.

Burying his hands in her hair and pulling hard, he never stopped pounding away inside her. Never let his body find its own release. Not until he made sure she found hers. And as mean as she was right now, coaxing sweet words wouldn't do it for her. Loving, affectionate touches would never get her there. There was only one thing to do.

Rubbing her clit with his pelvis with every thrust, Zach growled, "You better come for me, bitch. You better come for me right now or I'll leave you hanging there. Begging me to let you come. Begging me to send you over that edge."

"You son of a bitch!" She slammed her fists hard against him. A human male would have had destroyed shoulder blades, but Zach sneered and yanked her head back, forcing her to look up at him.

"Do it, Sara. Come." He licked her neck. It tasted perfect. So he fit his teeth right below her ear.

"Come, Sara. Come or I'll make you regret it." He bit down and that was it.

Her entire body bowed under him, arching off the mattress, nearly shoving him to the floor. Her hands grabbed hold of his shoulders, fingers digging deep as her legs wrapped around his waist and held on tight.

Screaming and sobbing, she came hard. Her body rocking against his, her pussy clamping down and holding Zach inside her.

Finally, Zach let himself come and as soon as he let go, a second wave rocked through her. It felt like their release went on and on, their bodies locked in battle until they could no longer move.

When Zach could once again function, he pushed himself up on one elbow and looked down at Sara's face. Her eyes opened and he saw all that feral lust had disappeared. At least for the moment.

She gave a soft smile and fell back asleep.

Zach gently pushed Sara's sweat-soaked hair off her face and kissed her nose. "I am so in over my head with you, aren't I?"

As if in answer, Sara turned on her side but not before shoving him off with one good push. By the time he hit the floor, she was snoring.

Chapter Fifteen

Sara finally opened her eyes. At first she wasn't quite sure where she was. But she quickly realized it was her bedroom, in her house—with one large arm thrown possessively over her waist.

Tell me I didn't. But she knew she had. It all came flooding back to her...sort of—the club, the bar fight, that bitch Casey. And the best sex she'd ever had in her life.

Frowning in thought, *Maybe even twice?*

She didn't know. She couldn't remember. At least when she lost it, she really lost it.

She looked over her shoulder at Zach. Out cold, his dark brown hair fell across his face, but she could still see the bruises and cuts from the bar fight.

Sara couldn't believe that was her last night. She'd been completely out of control. Although, the more she thought about it, the more she realized she hadn't been out of control—at least not in the usual sense. In fact, she'd been completely aware of every move she'd made. Almost hyper-aware.

She glanced over at the clock on her night table. Still had a couple of hours until she had to be into work, but she simply couldn't face Zach when he woke up. He would, naturally, think her a big ol' slut. Probably want to pass her around to his friends. She couldn't really blame him. She didn't merely throw herself at the guy. She practically tackled him. The thought made her cheeks burn.

She carefully slipped out from under his arm and off the bed, her entire body feeling sore and deliciously used. Throwing on some clothes she left lying on the floor, she quietly—and quickly—escaped her own house.

CR CR CR

Zach knew the minute she woke up. He felt her whole body tense up. She slid out of bed, got some clothes, and was gone.

Part of him wanted to stop her. Grab her fine ass and drag her back to bed—he wasn't near being done with that body. But he was too busy kicking himself in the ass. She was his. Even if she had no intention of letting him near her again, no other woman would ever get close to him. He wouldn't let them. Bound to her for the rest of his life, the realization did not make him happy. Forget he never wanted this in the first place. Forget he was convinced she might be clinically insane and definitely feral. The bottom line was, she ran. She didn't kiss him awake or make him breakfast. She didn't even stop to shower. She woke up, saw Zach lying next to her, and took to the Texas hills. Not a good sign when one was just starting out in a relationship.

Zach turned over with a sigh and looked up at the ceiling. "You are an idiot, Sheridan."

CR CR CR

Sara unlocked Miki's apartment door with her key. They each had a set of the others' keys for safety reasons. Theory was it was for emergencies only; otherwise, you knocked. This definitely constituted as an emergency.

She found Angelina asleep on Miki's incredibly comfy couch and Miki asleep in the recliner. Neither moved when she walked in, so she slammed the door shut. Angelina didn't move, but one eye opened and focused on Sara. Miki, however, flew out of the recliner, the book she still had in her hand raised as a weapon.

Sara looked at her two closest friends. "Well...I'm a whore."

"Oh, please." Angie closed her eyes again and turned over.

Miki seemed equally unimpressed. "Not again." Miki threw her book on the old coffee table. "Give us a break. And what the fuck happened last night anyway? We leave you alone for two minutes and you up and disappear on us."

"We were worried sick," Angelina added from the couch; her voice muffled because she buried her head into the cushions.

"I just went for a walk. *Then things spun out of control!*" Sara yelled the last sentence.

"Skelly called last night. He's unbelievably pissed at you. He said to tell you that you are going to pay for the repairs and he's debating whether to bar your ass."

Sara didn't blame the man, she felt like the whole thing was her fault.

"So are you going to tell us what happened or not?" This from muffled-Angelina.

"I need a shower first."

Miki took a step back. "You haven't showered?" She pointed an accusing finger. "You're still covered in his DNA, aren't you?"

Sara started to say something, and then thought better of it. She needed her friends right now. Instead, she stalked off to the bathroom, while Miki and Angelina burst out laughing.

"And throw out the soap when you're done!"

Once clean enough for Miki's standards, Sara changed into sweats she had left over at Miki's and filled her friends in on the last sixteen hours, while they ate bacon and eggs cooked by Angelina. Although Sara remained extremely sketchy on the fuck-of-a-lifetime details.

"So basically," Angelina analyzed, "you were the bone and they were the dogs fighting over it...uh...you."

"I am really starting to hate your analogies."

"Whatever. And his cock was huge?"

Miki choked out past a piece of toast, "So don't need to hear that."

"Enormous." Sara held her hands up to give an approximate length.

"Rock on." Angelina gave the thumbs-up and pushed herself off the couch. "I need coffee. Anyone else?"

Both Sara and Miki nodded and Angelina moved off to the tiny kitchen right next to the tiny living room.

"Still hungry?" Miki asked quietly as Sara sopped up the last of the egg yolk with her toast. Sara shrugged. She could eat a ton of bacon and never get full. She loved bacon. Miki's eyes narrowed as she studied her friend. "Perhaps you'd like a steak? Rare?"

Sara put her plate down on the coffee table. "Uh...no. Why?"

Miki shook her head. "No reason."

"Okay." Sara knew that tone—years and years of experience. "What's going on?"

"Well, we have a theory."

"No," Angie called from the kitchen. "*We* do not have a theory. *You* have a theory."

"Whatever," Miki snapped back. "It's just that I've been analyzing the situation." *Uh-oh.* "And based on your recent body change—"

"Body change?"

"Increased muscle mass, tone and strength."

Sara looked down at herself. She *had* liked the shape of her abs this morning when she was showering.

"And increased senses."

"Senses?"

"We practically had to leave the apartment to have a discussion you couldn't hear."

"You mean when you went into the bedroom? No. I heard you clear as crystal and my feet are not inordinately big."

"Not if you're a man," Angie interjected.

"Shut up."

"Mhhm. Interesting. You could hear us." Sara could see Miki clicking off some checklist firmly planted in her head.

"Increased aggression."

"I'm not aggressive."

"Maybe we should ask Casey about that." Wow, Miki could be smug. How did she never notice that before?

"She looked at me funny."

"Uh-huh." Check. "Increased sexual drive." Sara opened her mouth to protest that one, but Miki cut her off. "When I asked you how you felt yesterday, your response to me was, 'Horny. Very, very horny'."

"Oh. Yeah. I did say that, didn't I?" Check. "And what does all that prove, Dr. Psychopath?"

Miki folded her arms in front of her chest. All she needed now was the lab coat. "Werewolf."

Sara choked out a laugh. She couldn't help herself. "Have you lost your mind?"

"I have proof."

"What proof?"

Miki handed her the book she'd thrown on the coffee table earlier that morning. Sara read the title out loud, "The Truth About Werewolves?"

"Really good book. Factual. It's all in there."

"That's your proof?" Sara threw the book down. "All right. No more reading for you."

Sara went into the kitchen. She grabbed several more pieces of bacon and hopped on to the counter using only her legs. Angelina looked at her from the corner of her eye. "That's new."

"Cool, huh? Must be my new superpowers."

"You keep joking, stretch," Miki snapped. "But wait until the next full moon."

Sara looked at Angelina. "Full moon?"

"Don't worry." Angie pulled coffee mugs out of the cabinet. "You've got a good three weeks before that happens."

"When your body starts morphing at the full of the moon—don't call me." Miki disappeared into her bathroom.

"We've got to get her out of that bookstore."

"Wouldn't help." Angie pulled milk from the refrigerator and set everything up on the counter beside Sara. Staring at the coffee maker, they both waited for the dark liquid like it was elixir from the gods. "Are you still going to work today?"

"Yeah. Why?" Sara knew where this conversation was going.

"Just wondering…" Sara waited for it. She wasn't disappointed. "…if you'll be seeing Zach."

"I don't know. I doubt it. I don't know." Christ, she sounded like an idiot.

Angelina smiled softly. "He loves you, you know." That wasn't what Sara expected. Not by a long shot.

She burst out laughing again. "Oh, my God. You're crazier than Miki is."

"But you know I'm right." Angie pulled the glass pot out of the coffee maker and poured two mugs full of the steaming brew. She handed one to Sara.

"Look, Ang, he came over, he fucked me. I'm pretty confident that's the extent of our relationship."

Angie shook her head. "He didn't 'come over.' Skelly told us everything. He came there to get you. He was looking for you, Skelly heard that blond guy on the phone with him. And he protected you from that girl Casey. He fought for you, Sara."

Sara stared down at her mug of coffee. "I can't believe that right now." Putting the untouched coffee down on the counter, she slipped off.

"Why not?"

Sara headed to the front door, snatching up her backpack on the way. "Because when he leaves, it'll kill me." She opened the door, but looked back once at her friend. "And you said it yourself. He will leave."

Sara had gotten down the stairs of the apartment complex when she heard Angelina's voice from above her. "Sara." Sara stopped at the foot of the stairs and turned back to her friend.

"You're right. He's going to leave. But whoever said he'd leave without you?"

Without waiting for Sara to answer, Angelina turned and went back into the apartment.

Chapter Sixteen

The conversation with Angelina kept replaying through her mind. He couldn't love her. Not somebody like him. And she absolutely refused to love him. It didn't matter how gorgeous he was or how well he fucked. What did matter was that she just didn't have any faith in love or lovers or people who said they were in love or any of it. So, she wasn't about to be led down that path. Not for anything or anybody. Especially not for Zach. Never for Zach.

"Hi."

"Nothing!" she snapped for no reason in particular.

Conall stood there, staring at her. Appearing a tad concerned.

"Everything okay?"

Sara took a breath. "Just fine."

"Good. Where's Marrec?"

Sara motioned to the back room with a nod. Conall headed in that direction. "Is it just you today?" he asked, almost innocently.

Sara bit the inside of her mouth to stop from smiling. "Yeah. Just me."

Shrugging, he disappeared in the back. Sara grinned. That boy had it bad for her brutally honest friend. Poor thing. Miki would eat him for breakfast.

"What a beautiful smile you have."

Again Sara was startled out of her thoughts, but she had no idea who this was. He was handsome enough. Tall, powerfully built, golden blond hair, green eyes, and clothes straight out of GQ.

Still she should call Angelina, because he wasn't doing a thing for her.

"Thanks." Sara went back to her magazine. She figured the guy only wanted to look around to say he had. He didn't exactly seem like the Harley-Davidson type.

"I smell him all over you," he whispered. "Did he fuck you well, little girl?"

Sara felt her mouth go dry and a jolt of fear slip down her spine. But she controlled it. Slowly, oh so slowly, she looked up into those beautiful, cold green eyes. Smiled. And punched the prick in his face. The man's head snapped back, but he seemed more surprised than hurt. Then he looked pissed. He grabbed Sara by the throat and hissed, "Dog's whore." Which seemed an odd turn of phrase. Yet before Sara could react to it or this stranger's hand on her throat, she heard a growl coming from behind her.

It was Conall. The big, sweet bear chasing after her friend a few minutes ago was gone, and in his place stood a man who on a dark night she'd cross the street to avoid. Behind him, Marrec, and Sara couldn't remember ever seeing him so angry or dangerous looking. But it was the growl coming from the front door that completely shocked her.

He stood there. Beautiful as ever, frothing with rage. Zach's hazel eyes almost black, his lips curled back as he snarled his obvious displeasure. Sara was torn between being scared to death and wanting to fuck his brains out.

The stranger looked back at her and their eyes locked. His hand tightened on her throat ever so slightly. "I do hope he's not too attached to you," was all he said. Then he pulled her close and forced his mouth on hers. Sara screamed and grabbed his face, digging her nails into the tanned flesh, trying to hurt him enough so he'd release her. The kiss lasted only a few seconds, then he was gone. Over the bikes and out the side door. Zach and Conall went after him while Marrec came to stand beside her.

"*Who the fuck was that?*" Sara screamed while she repeatedly wiped her hand over her mouth.

"A problem," Marrec answered. Then the man who practically raised her did something that was going to freak Sara out for the rest of the night. He sniffed her. "Oh, boy," he sighed. "Zach's gonna kill him." With that, he turned and disappeared back into his workshop.

At that moment, things just got too weird for her. What did Miki say? Werewolf?

Sara grabbed her backpack and left.

ରେ ରେ ରେ

They tracked him to the forest. Once safely protected by the trees, Zach and Conall ripped off their clothes, shifted, and tore after the bastard they were tracking. They caught sight of him heading through the trees and up an embankment. He, too, had shifted, moving fast through the forest. Zach circled around while Conall went straight for him.

The prick charged up one of the old trees, but the branch he jumped on wasn't sturdy. It broke and he fell. Landing on his feet, he took off again, but he'd lost precious seconds. Zach latched on to his leg while Conall went for his neck. The big cat wasn't going down without a fight, though. He slashed at Conall, ripping into his muzzle before he could get to the soft flesh of his throat. But Conall kept coming. So he spun on Zach, but Zach wouldn't let go. Not with the bastard still having Sara's smell on him. He was going to kill him. But they were near the edge of the embankment. When Conall tackled the cat to get at his throat, their combined weight pushed Zach back to the edge. He saw Conall snap the cat's neck just as he lost his footing. The ground gave way, and Zach's body slid down the hillside.

The last thing he heard before hitting the ground was Conall screaming his name.

ભ ભ ભ

Sara's pickup truck arrived at her house well after midnight. She'd headed over to Angelina's house when she left the shop. She knew she couldn't go to Miki's. Tell her Marrec had begun sniffing people, and all hell would break loose.

So, instead, she and Angelina drank iced tea, watched the sunset from the porch, and obsessed over what the hell might be happening in their tiny town. Raves. Strange bikers. Guys randomly attacking shop girls. It was simply getting weirder and weirder every second.

Angelina offered to let her crash at her place, but Sara wanted to go home. Besides, she had her basic home defense, so she wasn't too worried. Still, Angelina insisted she take her shotgun to keep in the truck, worried about Sara just getting to her house safely. Not surprising, considering the last few hours.

Sara jumped out of her pickup and landed on both feet. It took her a second to realize she felt no pain. Perhaps the most glorious feeling in the universe. She couldn't get too worried about her weird life when her body felt so wonderful.

She grabbed her backpack, leaving Angelina's gun in the gun rack—*I do love Texas*—and slammed her truck door by doing a little spin and bumping it with her hip.

It caught her attention as she headed toward her front door. Laid out on its side, taking up half the length of the porch. At first, Sara feared it was dead, but as she got closer, she saw its chest and side rise with each breath. So, moving slowly, she went up her porch steps and stared.

She remembered now. The wolf who had stared at her the other day. Holy shit the fucker was huge! A good two hundred pounds or so. Probably more. The largest dog she ever owned was about one-hundred-and-twenty-five pounds, and when he dragged her across a riverbed to catch a rabbit, she decided never anything that large again.

Leaning down, she ever-so-gently touched his back paw. No movement, and she could see the deep gash on his side, his fur matted with blood and dirt.

Briefly, Sara debated whether to go back to her truck to get Angelina's gun, but instead cautiously moved around him and, after quickly unlocking the door, went into her house. She grabbed the phone and dialed four-one-one. She eventually got through to animal control, but they immediately put her on hold. While she waited and watched the wolf from her porch, she saw headlights heading up the path to her house. She watched until they disappeared. Just like that, which meant someone shut them off to avoid being seen. Probably not good.

"Shit," Sara got out as Angie's concerns and the day's past events flooded her mind. Stuffing the cordless phone into her back pocket, she nearly slammed the door shut, leaving the wolf to fend for himself, but for some completely irrational reason, she couldn't. She felt she had to protect him.

"Fuck. Fuck. Fuck."

She ran to her closet and grabbed the muzzle she'd used for her largest dog, Rocks, and her own always-loaded pump-action shotgun. She went back to the wolf. His eyes still closed, he seemed to be out cold. Burying all her fear, and any logical thought, she carefully knelt beside him, placing the shotgun at her feet. She put the metal basket muzzle on him, tightening the leather strap that would hold it in place should the wolf try to take her arm off. She grabbed him under the shoulders and dragged him into the house. It should have been harder, but…well, maybe he wasn't as heavy as she originally thought. Once she had him settled, she went back out to her porch and retrieved her gun.

An extremely expensive car pulled up to the front of her house and four men got out. All well-built and all well-dressed. Okay. The guy in the shop seemed to have brothers. Not a problem. The four men began to head toward the house, but she pumped the weapon once and aimed at the first one she saw. They stopped moving. They may have even stopped breathing.

"You're trespassing. Get off my property."

The one she had her weapon aimed at decided he would charm her. She saw it in the way his eyes half closed and his mouth held a small smile. He acted like he already owned her ass. But when he opened his mouth to speak, Sara shot the ground at his feet. All four men stumbled back.

"Welcome to Texas, gentlemen. Now get the fuck off my property!"

They dove into their car and were gone.

Sara took her phone out and quickly dialed.

"Sheriff's Office," a deep voice drawled. "Deputy Fogle speaking."

"Hey, Eddie. It's Sara Morrighan."

"Hey, darlin'. How you doin'?"

It was true, Sara had always been a sucker for the cowboys and the cops. But her weakness and general kindness to them also helped her. Like right now.

"I'm not bad. I was wondering, though, if you and your boys could do me a favor tonight. Some strangers were round my property just a few minutes ago. Never seen 'em before. *Not from around here*, if you know what I mean?"

"We've been seeing a lot of that in town the last couple of weeks." *I just bet you have.*

"Well, I was wonderin' if y'all could check my house from time to time tonight and make sure they don't come back."

"For you, Sara Morrighan? That's not a problem. I do hope you gave them strangers a Texas-sized welcome."

Sara laughed. "I sure did. But I gotta sleep sometime. Be nice to know you guys will be watchin' my back."

"You bet. I'll send a car out there right now."

"Thanks, Eddie. Tell the sheriff I said hey."

"Sure will. You sleep well now."

Sara turned off her phone, looked out again into the darkness, and finally went back inside. She locked and bolted her door.

She stared down at her wolf friend still out cold on her floor. Once again, irrational behavior took over. She hauled the poor thing up on to her couch, cleaned off his wound, realized it wasn't as deep as it initially looked, and wrapped it in a clean bandage. Then, to top it off, she covered him with a blanket.

Yup, I am clearly losing what is left of my mind. Soon I'll be as crazy as my grandmother.

Sara made sure all her doors and windows were locked, took a shower and went to bed.

Chapter Seventeen

Three a.m. and Sara still couldn't fall asleep. All that obsessing over *everything* did not make for a good night's rest. Well, it started off obsessing over everything until swinging around to obsess exclusively over Zach. He looked so angry when he saw that scumbag touching her. He actually snarled. Snarled! It was kind of cool.

"This is ridiculous." Sara tossed the covers aside and slipped out of bed. She padded out of her bedroom, through the hallway, through the living room, into her kitchen. She poured herself a glass of ice cold water and headed back to her bedroom. She'd just gotten to the hallway when she stopped dead in her tracks, the glass of water gripped tight in her hand. Eyes staring straight ahead, Sara slowly walked backward until she was standing in her living room. Taking a deep breath, she turned her head until she looked directly at the couch. And there he was, laying on it. His wound bandaged. The blanket she'd placed over him pushed down so it rested around his hips. The muzzle still on his face.

She stared at him. Just stared.

After a few moments, his eyes opened. Looking around in confusion, he pushed the muzzle off his face, and frowned at it. Then his eyes focused on Sara.

"Sara?"

"Zach?"

Several seconds slipped by, then he said, "Wait—"

She didn't. Her water hit the floor and she bolted. He was off the couch, charging after her. She ran into the dining room and around the large oak table, Zach a second behind her. He stood naked on one side of the table while Sara stood on the other. She took two steps to the left. He shadowed her. She took three quick steps to the right. He did the same.

"You…you're…" She couldn't even think straight.

"I need you to remain calm."

"Fuck you!"

"That's not calm."

Sara growled.

"Okay. Okay." Zach held his hands up, fingers spread wide. "I know you're confused. And scared. But everything's cool. Give me five minutes, I can explain everything to you."

"You can explain to me why last night I went to bed with a big shaggy dog on my couch and four hours later I find you? You can explain that to me?"

Zach went silent for a moment. "You're right. Why bother?" He lunged across the table for her. Sara stumbled back and slammed against the wall behind her. He missed her, so Sara jumped onto the table, over him, and tore across the room. But he was so fast. She'd made it to the hallway when she felt his arm grab her around the waist. She struggled desperately, trying to get away from him, but he continued to easily control her with one arm.

She screamed in frustration and kept screaming. Zach brought his other hand up to cover her mouth, but Sara saw it coming. Grabbing his arm, she wrapped her mouth around his flesh, and bit down. He grunted in pain but that was all. She bit harder but still he made no sound. Now she was getting pissed. She wanted to hear him scream. That's when she felt it—her canine teeth grew. Just like that they burst from her gums. The other teeth in her mouth re-adjusted to accommodate the canines' new length and they easily sank deep into his flesh.

Zach pulled her tight against him and buried his face in her hair. "I hate to tell you this," he muttered, his voice thick in what Sara assumed was pain. "But we consider what you're doing foreplay. You're making my dick hard."

Startled by his admission, her canines immediately retracted and she felt the rest of her teeth adjust back to their old position.

Then Zach lifted her like a load of laundry and carried her into the bathroom. He looked around, seemed satisfied she couldn't get out through the tiny, high window, and tossed her into the tub.

Sara's ass hit the hard linoleum. "Ow!"

He didn't even look at her, instead grabbing a towel and wrapping it around his waist. Then he slammed the bathroom door closed and opened her medicine cabinet. Pulling out alcohol and bandages, he ran his bleeding arm under the faucet.

"You know, this is why I didn't tell you earlier. I knew you wouldn't be rational."

Sara wiped Zach's blood off her mouth with the sleeve of her football shirt. "What did you do to me?"

"Nothing. You are what you are without my help."

"What does that mean?"

Zach poured rubbing alcohol over his wounded arm. "It means I didn't *do* anything to you. You just didn't know what you were. You can actually blame your parents for what you are."

Sara took a large, dramatic breath. "I am a werewolf then?"

Zach looked at her as if she were insane. "There's no such thing as werewolves."

Sara stood up, her aggression coming off her in waves. She could feel it. Two more seconds and—feral! "Then what the hell are you?"

"A shapeshifter." He seemed truly insulted. Like she'd called him cracker or redneck or said his mother wore combat boots. "The whole Pack are shifters. So was my father. And his father. And on and on. I can trace both my father and mother's families back to the druids. Werewolves," he spat out in disgust as he turned back to his wound. "And at night the boogeymen come and get us."

"Don't give me attitude."

"Then don't ask me stupid questions." He readjusted the bandage on his arm. "This isn't about things that go bump in the night. It's about a gift handed down to us through the ages. I live my life in this world and theirs. And I wouldn't change it for anything."

"You're a freak."

"Yeah. Probably. But I'd take one of us over what you'd call normal. At least I always know where I stand with them."

He may know where he stood, but she was completely lost. "Why are you here, Zach?"

"It involves me falling off one of those goddamn hills you're so proud of, but that's a very long story."

"Why are you *here*?" She didn't mean tonight. She meant at all.

Zach understood.

"Your parents were part of our Pack. But we had to wait until that old bitch died before we could come for you." Zach tied off his bandage.

"So last night—"

He brutally cut her off, "Don't even go there. I didn't have to fuck you last night."

Sara winced, but stood her ground. "That's good to know. I'd hate to think you were just following orders."

"Wait."

Sara hadn't moved, but he seemed to think she was about to. "That's not what I meant to say." Zach touched Sara's arm. She looked down at his big, strong hand. She'd gotten finger-fucked with that hand.

She didn't even know she was going to do it until her fist actually made contact with his jaw. His head snapped to one side, but he swung back with a snarl and Sara took a step farther into her tub, away from him. His canines extended and his hazel eyes glinted in the dim bathroom light.

"Holy shit." Then she had her finger in his mouth—she couldn't help herself. He stopped and stared at her as her forefinger ran over the white enamel. "That's so cool. Now I remember why I've been so obsessed with your teeth. Do mine look like that?"

Zach pulled her finger out of his mouth. "You're crazy."

She stepped out of the tub and went to the bathroom mirror. She raised her lip and carefully examined her face.

"What are you doing?" Zach seemed almost afraid to ask.

"Seeing what my scary wolf face looks like."

Putting his palms against his eyes, he sighed—deeply. A cleansing sigh really. Somehow Sara knew that with a little effort she could make him do that all the time.

"You can't stay here," Zach suddenly announced.

"Why?"

"They're after you. Remember the guy who attacked you today in the shop?"

"It was more like a kiss." She heard Zach growl but kept her face completely neutral. *Fuck him.*

"Whatever. But he's one of several. Like the guys at the club that first night I was here. He's Pride."

"You mean proud."

There was that sigh again. "I mean he's *Pride.*" That stated through gritted teeth.

"Pride? Lions have prides."

"Yup."

Sara spun around. "There are lions, too?"

Patient Zach made an entrance. "Yes. And tigers. And mountain lions. There's an array of shifters."

"Bunnies?"

Sara watched him swallow. "No bunnies," he bit out. Much more and he'd grind his teeth into dust. "Think predators. Our ancestors became one with the predators. Bunnies are low on the food chain."

"Sharks?"

"*What?*"

"Don't get huffy. They're the ultimate killing machine."

"I can't have this conversation." He leaned against the bathroom wall.

"Zach?"

Another sigh. "Yes?"

"How many are in a Pride?"

He shrugged. "Ranges. But about eight or nine."

"Male and female?"

"Yeah."

"And they killed my parents?" She watched Zach's face soften and he nodded. "And now they're here for me." Again Zach nodded.

With that she was out the bathroom door.

He never thought she would run. And he was right. She didn't. Instead she grabbed the well-oiled shotgun leaning against the hallway closet. He smelled gun powder and realized she'd recently fired it. Snatching a box of ammo from the top of a bookshelf, she moved straight to the front door.

Zach caught her in his arms before her hand reached the doorknob. But she was in full aggression mode and easily pulled out of his grip. She swung the shotgun back, aiming for his head.

Instinctively he caught the weapon before it struck him; although the human side of him was startled and a little hurt she would attack him. Luckily he wasn't depending on that side of himself to stay alive.

"Christ! What is your damage?" he snapped while trying to pull the gun away from her.

"They were here."

That stopped him. In fact, it froze him to the very spot where he stood. "What?"

"They were here," she repeated. "Probably looking for you. And I let them go. I should've killed them. I should've killed them all."

"How many?"

"I don't know." She pulled at the weapon, trying to get it out of his grasp. "Three. No. Four."

"Females?"

"No. Males. Give it!"

Zach let the weapon go and Sara, surprised he let it go so abruptly, stumbled back. The only thing stopping her ass from hitting the floor, the old chair she fell into.

"And that's the only reason you're still breathing," he snarled. "You, and your little gun, wouldn't have meant much against four Pride females."

Zach rubbed his tired eyes. "Stupid. I led them right here."

"You're an idiot."

Zach took a deep breath and looked at the only woman he would—tragically!—ever love. "Why?"

"Because you didn't *lead* them here. They already knew where I lived. I think they were the ones who attacked my truck the other day. Since they smelled you on me—ewww, by the way—they probably just figured you'd come here. Now move." She stood up. "I gotta kill some cats."

One minute she was completely logical. The next a raving lunatic. She really just plucked his last goddamn nerve.

Snatching the shotgun from her, he tossed it across the room, praying it wouldn't hit the wall or floor and accidentally go off. The ammo followed right after.

She stood there in front of him with her baggy flannel pants, no shoes, and a Dallas Cowboy football shirt, itching to kick some Pride ass. He guessed it would just have to be his ass.

That was it. Sara was just going to have to kick his fine ass. Right here and right now.

Her fist reached back to punch him again and hopefully break his nose this time, when he grabbed her around the waist and lifted her off the floor. High enough she had to look down at him. Impressive. Not simply because he risked getting that close to her when even she could feel herself going feral again, but because at six feet tall and…well…rather "curvy", she wasn't the first chick guys looked at to lift over their heads—unless they were football players and seriously drunk.

"Do I have your attention now?"

His voice, so soft and so seductive—she should have known he was up to absolutely no good. Because when she nodded yes, Zach, with an evil-sounding "good" chucked her—yes, *chucked her*—across the living room into her old, but thankfully sturdy, couch.

Sara let out a surprisingly girlish squeal, landing on her side, her ass hitting the back cushions. To Sara's further astonishment she wasn't hurt, mostly stunned. When she opened her eyes, which she slammed shut as soon as she took flight, Zach was walking calmly toward her.

"Honestly. The things I have to do to keep you from killing anybody."

And there went the towel. The only thing between her and his mammoth cock.

She scrambled up onto all fours and tried to go over the armrest, but he grabbed her arm and swung her around to face him.

"Oh, no you don't, beautiful."

"Don't even think about it—aye!" He'd snatched her off the couch and wrapped her legs low around his waist, his hands under her ass and his lips on her throat. He pushed his hard erection against her leg and it all felt so freakin' good.

"Don't," she begged. "I can't think when your hands are on me."

"Good. Then we're even."

She started at that. Could she actually have the same effect on him that he had on her? She didn't want to believe it. Instead she wanted to hate him. Hate him for breaking through armor she'd spent her whole life building around herself so she could be safe.

He pulled at her jersey and she grabbed his hand. "Hey! There will be no yanking or tearing of the Cowboys. Ever."

First he looked surprised. Then he looked amused. "You better get it off then…or it's shredded."

Sara swallowed as she realized that as "amused" as he may look, he was as serious as a heart attack. At least she convinced herself that taking off her shirt would protect her Cowboys and not because she wanted his hand and mouth on her tits.

She leaned back and pulled the jersey over her head, dropping it to the floor.

"Now the pants." He placed her back on the couch so she stood over him, his hand still possessively on her hip.

"I—" was all she got out, but he tugged at her favorite comfy pants with an expression that said "either you take them off or I take them off".

"Okay. Okay. Christ, I'm runnin' out of clothes." She untied the drawstring and let the pants fall at her feet. She heard a definite change in his breathing as he stared at her body, his hand running over her flesh. Sara looked at the ceiling, completely uncomfortable with anyone staring at her naked. So many scars. So many flaws. No, no, he needed to look at something else right now. Right this minute!

"You going to look at me?" he asked softly.

"Nope."

He kissed her stomach. "You sure?"

She cleared her throat. "Yup."

"Okay. If that's what you want." His finger slipped inside her pussy.

Sara let out a surprised gasp as his thumb caressed her clit, while his forefinger slowly stroked in and out of her. She wanted to ignore him. Wanted to keep looking at the ceiling and pretending he wasn't giving her a hand job right in the middle of her living room. But when his middle finger joined the other inside her and his thumb made lazy circles around her clit, she couldn't pretend anymore. Her hands gripped his shoulders and her eyes locked with his.

Zach smiled at her. That sweet smile she had so grown to love. "Tell me what you want, Sara."

What she wanted? She closed her eyes. How was she supposed to know that? Five minutes ago, she wanted nothing more than to kill somebody. Now, at this very moment, she could care less. She didn't know what she wanted.

"I don't know."

"Liar." He licked a line across her belly. "Tell me what you want, Sara."

Warmth spread from her groin and up her back, blazing heat building. She held onto his shoulders, the only thing keeping her standing.

"You, Zach." She opened her eyes and looked down at him. "I want you."

Was that surprise on his handsome face? She wasn't sure. But a second later it disappeared, replaced by the hungry look of a predator. He kept working her clit, while his other two fingers slowly fucked her. She dug her own fingers into his shoulders as the first spasm tore through her. Sara gasped and let out a moan as she came.

Zach felt her orgasm when her tight pussy practically snapped his fingers in two during the first spasm. It was watching her beautiful face, though, that made it all worth it. Her eyes closed, her bottom lip gripped by one of her incisors. Add in that fucking amazing growling sound she made when she came and he was in wolf heaven.

She spasmed again and then her knees gave out. He made sure she dropped onto the couch as opposed to the floor. Her breath coming out in ragged gasps and her fingers still gripping his shoulders. He laid his hand gently on her mound until the spasms eased down.

Finally she loosened her grip on him. But, to his surprise, she wrapped her arms around his neck and leaned her forehead against his chest and holy shit, but did that feel good—and right. "When, exactly," she mumbled into his chest, "did I become such a fucking whore?"

Now Zach was completely confused. "What are you talking about?"

"Me. I'm a whore."

Zach wasn't sure if she wanted him to start calling her that during sex or if she was serious. Instead of potentially sending her spiraling into depression, he decided to go with her possibly being serious.

"Do you do this sort of thing with everybody in town?"

"No!" She glared up at him, completely insulted.

"Then you're not a whore. Psychotic? Absolutely. Whore? No. Now…" He brushed against her smooth, tight body as he stretched out on the couch, his erection standing at full attention, as the damn thing always seemed to do in her presence. "I think you've got some unfinished business here."

She frowned in confusion, so he motioned to his cock. "Hello? You didn't finish the job last night."

She smirked, her arms crossing in front of her gorgeous chest. "If I remember correctly, you practically ripped the hair out of my head getting me off it."

"I called rain check."

Sara exploded into laughter. She had the sweetest laugh and, unlike the entire Pack, actually found him funny. "You are so full of shit!"

"No. Really. I said," he covered his mouth with one hand, still smelling her scent on it, "rain check."

"That's funny, 'cause I thought I heard 'flip over'."

"I was *thinking* rain check?" he asked hopefully.

"Pathetic." She ran one long finger up the entire length of his shaft. "At least not all of you is as pathetic." Dragging her finger along the tip, she cleaned off the pre-come. He watched her slip that finger into her mouth and suck it clean. He clenched his jaw tight as she leaned into him, her naked body pressing against his. She swept her tongue around and across his nipple, placed her mouth against it and softly sucked. Zach felt the tension from the past day slip away as her tongue led a brutal trail down his chest and across his abs, stopping briefly to lick his recent wound. Reaching out with both hands, he gently touched her black hair, marveling at how beautiful it was. How beautiful she was.

When his dick slipped into her mouth and that evil tongue of hers swirled around the tip, he forgot about everything but her. The Pack. The Pride. The war. He forgot all of it as he became lost to the scent of her body, the feel of her mouth on him, the way the silky strands of her hair felt on his naked flesh. He wanted this to last forever, but his body couldn't hold out that long. Not when he looked down and saw his dick being sucked by the most beautiful woman he'd ever known. The woman he loved.

Zach, his body screaming toward orgasm, grabbed Sara's head in both hands and roughly fucked her mouth. She didn't get mad. She laughed, her lips smiling around his dick and her hands gripping his thighs until his come flooded her mouth, and he let out a roar that shook the couch.

As the last spasm rippled through him, Zach laid back and tried to remember his name. Sara moved back up his body, kissing him as she went along. He felt her tongue slide across his neck and over his jaw. Then her lips were on his and he gripped her to him. He tasted himself when she sucked on his tongue and he immediately got hard again.

She pulled away from his kiss and looked down at his dick nudging at her sex. "Hold it!" Suddenly Zach was staring at her crotch as she bent over him to grab at her backpack. And since he was there anyway…

"Hey!" That after his tongue darted out and swiped her clit. "Cut that out." But she didn't sound half-convincing. She lowered herself to his lap and handed him the box of condoms.

He looked at it and smiled. "You do know you just licked my very recently opened wound?"

"So? Oh God, what's wrong with you? Mange?"

"There's nothing a therapist couldn't cure."

She nodded knowingly. "You could use a good therapist."

"I was talking about you."

Sara whipped that middle finger out like she might fast-draw a gun. "Besides, it's not disease I'm worried about." She leaned close to him, her face filled with the most serious expression he'd ever seen from her. "The fact is, I don't want children. Ever. And when I'm thirty, I'm gettin' fixed."

Zach frowned and leaned back. Could he have heard her correctly? She didn't want children? Ever? She didn't pine to be a mother? To know the joy of childbirth? Blah, blah, blah?

He grabbed her tight by the shoulders and stared straight at her. "My God, woman, I've been waiting for you all my *life*!" Startled by his shout, Sara reared back and fell off the couch.

"Shit, are you okay?" Zach looked down at her as she raised herself up on her elbows.

"What the fuck was that?"

"That…" he quickly slipped the condom on and was off the couch and between her legs, "…was utter fucking joy. That's what *that* was." He kissed her neck, her breasts, sucked on her earlobes.

Sara laughed at his loving onslaught. "You're insane."

Zach grabbed her waist and yanked her down while he thrust forward. His dick slammed into her and Sara stopped speaking. He was going to fuck the hell out of her and he just wanted her to enjoy it. He didn't want her to think about another goddamn thing while he was inside her.

Zach pulled back and slammed into her again. He marveled at how wet and tight she was. How sweet she smelled. And he loved that she wasn't into "nice". Because he had no real idea how "nice" worked. He equated "nice" to "boring" and neither of them were boring in his book.

Sara's bit into the lower part of his neck where his throat and collarbone met, her hands ripping ribbons of skin from his back. But he didn't mind. He barely felt it. Besides, every time she bit into him or tore flesh from him, she marked him as her own. Forever. Whether she meant to or not.

When her hands dug into his ass and she bit down into his shoulder—canines pushing through to ensure he couldn't get away—he buried himself inside her, pumping into her hot, wet pussy. The sounds of her moans and growls filled his senses, making him love her more and more. When he clamped his canines onto the side of her breast, her pussy clenched his cock into a vise-like grip as the first orgasm hit her.

He could have come then. Could have let her go, but he wasn't about to. He wasn't nearly done with her.

Sara knew she had to be causing him some serious pain. He bled from several spots on his neck, and under her fingernails she had flesh once belonging to his back. But every time her canines extended and tasted his flesh and blood, he slammed into her harder. She was turning him on, and everything about him made her wetter, hotter. Every time he said her name in her ear or against her flesh, she clenched, taking him deeper inside her.

When she came, she thought he'd come too and they'd lay around and do that "afterglow" thing Angie always talked about. But he didn't come. Instead he kept going. Kept slamming into her with the same level of ferociousness she'd come to expect—hell, demand—of him. And when his hand slid across the old wound on her thigh, Sara gasped, her entire body tightening.

Zach stopped. "God, did I hurt you?"

"No." She shook her head and stared at him. She couldn't tell him, couldn't give him that much power. That sort of thing could make a girl like her into some guy's love slave. Unfortunately, Zach read her like a book. He glanced down at her leg, his hand hovering right above it. With the lightest of touches, he ran his finger across the damaged flesh, and Sara grabbed his hand, her entire body jerking in response.

She couldn't explain it, but her old wound had somehow become a giant G-spot on her leg. Those fucking cats had somehow given Zacharias Sheridan the keys to the kingdom—namely her—and now Zach knew it. She received no comfort from the evil grin he gave her.

And when he pinned her hands above her head with one hand, she knew she was in serious trouble. Using his free hand, he slowly moved across her thigh, moved along the ridges left by those who'd tried to kill her as well as the paw marks he'd made a few days before. Sara's body arched in response, her pussy flooded.

Zach watched her face and she couldn't hide the pleasure he gave her. Not with her thighs clamping tight around his waist, ready to snap the man in half—the sensations almost too much to bear. She tried to pull her arms out of his iron grip, though she couldn't guarantee once her hands were free whether she'd knock him off her or simply rip more flesh from his back.

He began to fuck her again, his hand relentlessly moving across her old wound. Trapped while he basically forced unbearable pleasure onto her. She'd kill him if it hadn't been the best fuck of her life.

It didn't take long for Sara to come again, and good thing the bastard had control over her hands. She came so hard she wasn't sure she wouldn't have torn his throat out or ripped his cock off. Instead she buried her teeth under his chin and bit down. His body jerked in response and then he was coming, right behind her, slamming his cock into her, his hand gripping the flesh of her thigh.

They both screamed out, the last spasm shaking them. After a few moments or years…whatever…Zach leaned back and looked at her. "I'm *so* going to have fun with that," he taunted, his hand tapping the tender flesh of her thigh.

Sara rolled her eyes. "Prick."

ल ल ल

Zach shoveled another spoonful of Fruit Loops cereal with milk into his mouth. "It is *not* possible!"

"How do you know? Just because there's no proof to prove it, there's no proof to *dis*prove it either."

"You're trying to make me crazy, aren't you?"

"Not at all." Sara put her bowl down. "I'm just saying there could be bunny shifters."

"*There are no bunny shifters!*"

Shaking her head she accused, "You're a bunny bigot."

Zach threw his spoon back in the near-empty bowl. "And there is no such thing as bunny bigots."

"Bunny bigot," she accused again.

How exactly did he get here? Lying naked and stomach down on the living room floor beside a naked Sara Morrighan, bunny advocate?

"We're not having this discussion anymore."

"Is this you being all in charge?"

"Where you're concerned, I *am* in charge."

"Are you happy in your land of delusions? Are you king there?"

Zach had to work hard not to laugh. Christ, he really liked her a lot, and he didn't like many people.

She sighed. "Look, if you're going to be all bitchy and unreasonable about the bunnies..." Sara climbed up on his back, wrapping her arms around his neck and grinding her hot crotch against his tight ass. "I guess you'll have to find some other way to keep me occupied."

"You're damn demanding." Zach closed his eyes and did his best to control the lust stampeding through him. Good God but the woman worked him like no one ever had before. Just the way she touched him made him absolutely crazy.

She licked the back of his neck. "You know what I like about you?"

"What?" He really wished she'd stop grinding herself against him. The ability to think quickly slipping away with every move she made.

"That you're so easy to torture." She nipped his ear. "You're like a cranky Rottweiler."

Zach sat up abruptly, causing Sara to roll off his back and hit the floor. "Hey!"

"We need to get something straight right now." Zach faced her, pushing his hair out of his eyes. Pulling herself into a sitting position, she stared at him as he struggled not to look at her tits. Not easy when all he wanted to do was bury his face right between them. But this was important...really important.

"Do not—and I mean never—compare a wolf with a dog. We *hate* that."

Sara said nothing for a good long time, then she leaned forward, staring deeply into his eyes. "Arf."

She burst out laughing and fell back on the floor, legs kicking up like a ten-year-olds. The woman was silly, exasperating, and so damn beautiful his back teeth ached.

Rolling his eyes, Zach took firm hold of her legs and yanked her over to him.

"Ow! Rug burn, dude!"

Ignoring her, Zach slipped his hands under her back and lifted her off the floor. "Kiss me, lunatic."

She turned her face away. "No. You're mean to me."

"You haven't seen me mean." Leaning down he grasped her nipple between his lips and sucked hard. Sara's hands slapped against his shoulders, her head falling back and her body arching into his, pushing her breasts closer to his face.

Shit, where did he put those condoms? Without releasing her breast or her body, he quickly glanced around the room. Spotting a box under the couch, he picked her up and moved them both closer to the couch—still without releasing her breast. What could he say? He really liked having her nipples in his mouth.

Reaching out, Zach grabbed hold of the box and brought it over. He glanced up to find Sara'd raised herself up on her elbows and stared down at him, one eyebrow raised.

"What the hell are you do—"

He sucked her nipple hard and Sara's head fell back again, cutting off her question. "Oh, my God, that feels so fuckin' good."

He smiled to himself. He liked that he wasn't the only one out of control. He had the condom on in seconds and then he was inside her.

Damn, but her pussy was tight. Tight and hot and all his. He ground his hips against hers and Sara reached up blindly, her hands digging into his hair.

Wrapping her legs around his waist, she pulled herself up so their bodies rubbed together. "Do that again. Please, Zach."

"Kiss me first, you evil little tease."

Tilting her head to the side, Sara smiled seconds before her lips mated with his. They both moaned, their tongues swirling around each other.

Man, he was in way too deep. Lost in this erotic haze with a crazy woman who felt the compulsion to fight for the rights of non-existent bunny shifters.

Pushing her back to the floor, Zach ground his hips against hers again. Sara tore her mouth away and gasped loudly. He must be hitting her clit just right. *Nice.* What a piece of ass. An ornery, crazy piece of ass, but a piece of ass just the same.

He kissed her cheek, then said against her ear, "Come for me, you crazy bitch."

Her eyes closed tight, Sara grinned. "Arf, arf, arf." She exploded, screaming out her orgasm and probably scaring the poor full-blood wolves lurking around the woods. Before she even stopped convulsing, Zach began fucking her with long, deep strokes. He took his time, enjoying the feel of her muscles contracting around his dick. Good thing they'd eaten something to tide them over, because he had no intention of stopping anytime soon.

ର ର ର

Sara grabbed the bunny by the scruff of the neck and stood. She grinned. True, she'd actually been going for that baby deer, but it moved too fast and the bunny crossed her path.

She'd had no intention of going after anything. She only wanted some fresh air and to enjoy the morning with her body all sore and well used again. With water bottle in hand and her Dallas Cowboys jersey back on, she'd happily walked out to her back porch. Soon after, she saw him. Or her. She didn't know. All Sara knew was that there was a deer in her backyard and she was feeling mighty hungry all of a sudden. Dropping the water bottle, she'd gone after it, but it took off as soon as she moved off the porch. A few minutes later, the little bunny hopped by.

"And what are you going to do with that?"

Zach stood on her porch, his arms crossed over that mouth-watering chest. He was completely naked. Gorgeous naked guy standing on *her* porch at eight in the morning. *That's right. I rock!*

Holding the bunny up to show him, the furry thing wiggling around in her hand, she said with immense pride, "Look what I caught! And I didn't have to shift or anything."

"I see. And, again, what are you going to do with it now that you've caught it?"

Sara frowned. "I don't know. I hadn't thought about it. I only wanted to catch the bunny." She grinned and added, "And to see if it's—"

"Don't say bunny shifter to me, woman," he growled.

Fighting her smile, "Okay."

Zach's hazel eyes glanced around her backyard. Finally, he nodded to her left. "Throw him over there."

"What?" She looked at the empty space behind her. She didn't want to throw her prize away. He was *her* bunny. "Why?"

"Do it. Trust me."

Feeling a twinge of regret, Sara tossed the rabbit across her backyard. It landed on its feet and started to hop away. It should have moved faster, though. Those two wolves dashed out of the surrounding trees like lightning and tore the thing apart between them.

"Holy shit!" Sara stumbled back, almost falling on the ground. Shocked and completely grossed out, she stammered to Zach, "I can't...you can't expect me to...there is no way..."

Zach motioned toward the house, holding his hand out for her to grasp. "Come on, beautiful. We've gotta talk."

The two wolves trotted off, each with their own bunny half as a prize.

Oh, yeah. They really needed to talk.

∞ ∞ ∞

At least now it all sort of made sense. Zach had given her the quick Morrighan family synopsis, promising more when they weren't still covered in each other's DNA and panting from exertion because he'd fucked her in practically every room of the house. He told her about who and what she was. He explained how her aggression was normal since she'd never shifted. And that helped her understand her grandmother.

Even why the Pack didn't come after her sooner now made sense. Apparently several of them had come to the hospital while Sara was still in her coma. Her grandmother had taken them to the back of the hospital to "chat" and attacked them with her favorite blade. One Pack member took a hit in the shoulder, another in the back and a female got her face cut, taking off part of her ear. Lynette left them all alive, but told them never to come back. That the "bitch" was hers now.

The Pack understood what Sara always knew. She was no more than a bone to a vicious dog. Her grandmother would have killed her first before handing her over to the people she blamed for taking away her daughter.

No, none of this information changed how much she hated Lynette but, for the first time ever, Sara finally understood the old bitch. More importantly, she definitely understood herself and why she'd always felt like a freak. Because she was a freak. But she found herself liking that. A freakiness she could definitely get used to.

Of course now she had to apologize to Miki. She'd been damn near close to right. And there was no way she'd ever let Sara live that shit down.

Sara settled back against the headboard of her bed, gently running her fingers through Zach's hair, his dark head resting against her chest. She felt as if he was always meant to be there. Lying comfortably between her thighs, making that low growling sound that absolutely curled her toes while his hands slowly moved up and down her legs. She wanted his place to be there forever. But, she knew, eventually he would leave and she'd be on her own again, no matter what Angie said. Sara would be on her own just like always. She held no false hope that what they had was anything more than great sex. She couldn't afford to hope for anything more. She couldn't handle the disappointment.

"Do you ride?" he asked her.

She smiled, her fingers lightly sliding around his ear. "Not since I hit that barn."

Zach's hands paused on her flesh. "You hit a barn?"

"I had to avoid the cow."

Zach burst out laughing and Sara couldn't help but smile wider. She liked making him laugh. She got the feeling a lot of people didn't.

"Okay. Okay. I guess you'll have to ride with me. No bike for you."

Sara frowned in the darkness. What the hell was he talking about?

His hand began to move again against her flesh. Slowly, seductively, as if he simply enjoyed touching her. God, how she would miss that.

"Do me a favor," he sighed. "Don't bring a ton of shit with you. It's a long enough trip without having to worry about a bunch of bags."

Sara tensed and cleared her throat. "What are you talking about?"

"Don't panic, we'll send for the rest of your stuff."

She grabbed him by that glossy mass of dark brown hair and snatched his head back, glaring into his hazel eyes. "What are you talking about?"

"What do you think I'm talking about? You're coming with me." It wasn't a question, or even a demand. Merely a statement of fact.

"I…I didn't agree to that." Wait. Did she? Christ, she didn't scream, "I'll go anywhere you want!" while coming, did she?

Zach turned his big body over, but never left his place between her thighs. "There's nothing to agree to. You're mine."

"What? Like a dog? I don't think so."

He smiled in the face of her anger, placing his big arms on either side of her. He dragged his large body against hers until their eyes met. She took in a ragged breath, her pussy becoming moist and hot. *Christ, I am a horny dog*, she thought as she itched to grab his cock and never let go.

"You don't get it, do you? You're not in this alone. You belong to me, but I belong to you. Even before you marked me, I belonged to you…as much as it annoys the shit out of me."

"Marked you?"

He glanced down at his bandaged arm and she realized what she'd done. Not just on his arm but all over his body. The man looked like a used chew toy. Then she realized what he'd just said. "And you annoy the shit out of me, too. You're an asshole."

"And you're a psychotic bitch." His head dipped down and he dragged his tongue across her nipple, causing her back to arch. "But I'm pretty sure I could fuck that right out of you."

"Well..." Her hands grasped the headboard, her body stretching out underneath him, her legs inching farther apart. She stared at him in open challenge. "You can *try*. But I'm not holding out any hope."

He smirked at her. "Really?" Then he ran his hand across her wounded thigh and her body jerked in response.

Her hands tightened on the headboard and she shook her head. "Those fuckin' cats."

Chapter Eighteen

Yup, she could actually *hear* her phone vibrating and it was in the other room, buried in her backpack. She had to admit it, this whole freak thing—gettin' pretty cool.

"Either you shut it off or I break it in half."

Zach lay on his stomach, his arm thrown possessively over her naked waist, his face buried in the pillow. And clearly not real friendly when he first woke up.

Sara slipped out of bed and silently padded into the living room. She found her bag by the couch, the dog muzzle right next to it. She couldn't help but smile, remembering Zach having that thing on his face.

She found the phone buried, as usual, in the very bottom of her backpack. Pulling it out, she quickly answered it before the caller hung up.

"It's Miki," was the reply. And she knew just by the sound of her best friend's voice something was seriously wrong. "You better get to the shop. The cops are here and I saw an ambulance pulling away."

Sara hung up the phone and moved.

ষ ষ ষ

The slamming door woke him up for the second time that day. But the banging on the window an hour later actually made him move.

Zach literally dragged himself up and out of bed. He sleepwalked to the window and pulled the shades open. Conall stood on the other side. Leave it to his best friend to wake him from one of those great sleeps. The kind of sleep you only get after fucking the woman you love throughout her entire house.

Zach opened the window. "What?"

"We've got a problem. They went after Marrec this morning." Conall shoved Zach's saddlebags from his bike through the window. "Get dressed. And thanks for letting us know you weren't dead."

Zach stared at his friend, seriously confused. Then it all returned to him—that bastard touching his female, the fight, and the falling. The last thing he remembered was Conall calling his name, but not much else…except gunshots.

"I'm sorry." Zach pulled his jeans out of the bag. His friend didn't answer and he knew Conall must be seriously pissed. "But if it makes you feel any better, she put a muzzle on me last night."

Conall started laughing and didn't stop until they got to the hospital.

Sara was already there when the two men arrived. She glanced at Zach when he and Conall walked into the room, but quickly turned back to Marrec.

The look on her face said it all. She blamed herself for what happened. Blamed herself for bringing the Pride to Marrec's territory. Blamed herself for putting him and his Pack at risk.

Marrec, though, seemed to be seriously enjoying the attention of three beautiful women. Miki fluffed his pillows, Angelina read his medical chart and Sara held a water cup to his lips so he could drink. Zach and Conall exchanged glances. They both knew this was ridiculous. Marrec had clearly been attacked. Zach wouldn't—couldn't—deny that. Half his face and throat covered in bandages that needed changing, his hands bruised and torn. Put plainly, the man was a mess. But he was also Pack. In two days he'd be fine. At the moment, as bad as he looked, he probably only felt a dull ache.

Zach turned and tested the air. Marrec's Pack lurked around somewhere, probably the cafeteria. And Zach's Pack had just arrived. Unfortunately, Casey was with them. "Shit," he muttered to Conall.

Yates came in first, stopping in the doorway to observe Marrec. "Comfortable?" he asked with obvious amusement.

"A lot of pain," Marrec forced out.

"Oh, come on," Yates sneered in return.

Zach would have laughed too, except Sara was pushing the red and grey hair off Marrec's face. Balling his hands into fists, Zach wondered what it would feel like to beat the shit out of an old man.

Casey entered the room then, her females following behind. Sara didn't even look up. Zach smiled—she'd smelled Casey coming.

Moving across the room, Casey's attitude was one of complete dominance. Her females didn't follow. They stood back and waited. He knew Casey well enough to know she was about to show Sara exactly who was Alpha Female of the Magnus Pack and although Zach could step in, he wouldn't. He needed Sara to start fighting these battles on her own. Even the ones she would lose.

"Excuse me, honey." Casey grabbed Sara by her jacket and hauled her up and off the bed. Sara spilled water on the floor as she stumbled out of the way. Casey sat on the bed beside Marrec. "Oh, you poor, baby. Are you okay?"

The room grew quiet. Even Angelina and Miki weren't speaking, clearly too stunned. But they did take several steps back, the whole thing feeling a lot more dangerous than it probably was. Sara wasn't ready to take on Casey and, from what Zach could tell, Sara knew it.

Zach watched his woman take a deep breath and place the empty water cup down on a nearby table. She turned away from Casey and stared down at her sneaker-covered feet.

He saw the struggle on her face. Knew what she wanted to do. And knew what she could handle. He expected her to walk away, and she didn't let him down. She walked away...for about five feet. Then, with a snarl, she spun back around and grabbed Casey from behind. One hand in the woman's hair, the other grabbing the denim jacket she wore. Sara snatched her off the bed and slammed Casey, face first, into the wall. She yanked her back, leaving a splash of blood on the white paint, and slammed her again. Then Sara threw her. Across the room and out the door, an arc of blood slashing across Marrec's bed. Zach heard Casey hit the wall with a sickening thud.

Sara, growling low, started to go after her when Miki and Angelina, not Pack and not knowing better, jumped in front of her.

"Hey! Hey!" Miki pushed her friend back. "Sara, *no!*"

Sara halted in her tracks, staring at her friends as if debating whether to tear their throats out or not. Instead she took a deep breath and looked over their heads at Zach. He glanced at the rest of the Pack females and, to his growing pride, Sara picked up on it immediately. Her head snapped around and she nailed the four other women with one brutal scowl. "What are you bitches looking at?" she snarled.

Immediately they all looked at the floor, the door, the ceiling— everything and anything *but* Sara. Zach bit back a smile and thought about mounting her right there in front of everybody.

That's when Miki grabbed Sara's jacket and dragged his woman from the room, Angelina following after them.

Once gone, Yates went over to see the damage to his female. They all knew his time as Alpha Male was now over. And the man seemed relieved.

Conall shook his head and grinned. "Your woman is a major bitch."

Zach grinned back. "Isn't she, though?"

ભ ભ ભ

Sara let Miki drag her out the hospital and around the back; eventually stopping in the doctors' parking lot, the forest behind them. She *let her do it.* Sara couldn't quite believe how strong she'd gotten in only a few days.

Miki finally released her. *"What is going on with you?"*

Sara looked at her friends. Tired and worn from worry over Marrec, they wouldn't be up to hearing the truth. Hell, even Angelina wore sneakers and sweats. Matching Versace sneakers and sweats, but still.

So what exactly should Sara say here? *Apparently I'm Pack now and I was exerting my dominance. You wouldn't understand.* That would play well. These pushy, tiresome, sometimes psychotic women were her best friends. They had been there when no one else had. She didn't want to lose them, and she knew if she told them the truth she'd lose them forever. Wouldn't she?

"Nothing. I'm fine." Boy *that* was lame.

Angelina and Miki exchanged glances. Sara had a feeling whatever they were about to say to her had already been discussed between the two of them. Angelina leaned back against an expensive car with MD plates and smiled.

"Miki and I were reminiscing on the phone last night. I forgot how much my grandmother hated when I went over to your house. At the time, I couldn't understand why because she liked you so much. So I asked her. And she said it was because your grandmother was *lobo del diablo.* Roughly translated, 'devil wolf'. I figured it was my grandmother's way of calling Lynette a bitch because of the Church Bake Sale Incident of 1984. But it wasn't that, was it?"

Sara, staring down at her feet, shook her head. She couldn't face her friends. So, instead she studied her feet and marveled at how big they were. She wondered what they would look like furry.

"You've gotten really strong," Miki noted. "You threw that blonde chick around the hospital room like a rag doll. Which, by the way, was so many levels of cool."

"And that growling thing you've been doing lately," from Angelina.

"And the snarling," Miki added.

"Bottom line is," Angelina finished, "maybe they're not werewolves. But they're not quite human, are they?" The women locked eyes. "And neither are you?"

Scratching the back of her neck, Sara looked down at her feet again. "I…uh…"

"Why don't you tell her? Tell her what you are."

The friends spun around at the sound of a strange voice. She knew him—the man she'd shot at the night before. As before, his three friends were with him. All golden and beautiful and so cold Sara felt her stomach drop. Why, oh, why hadn't she killed them?

"Hello, pretty. Now, why don't you be a good little puppy and come with us."

"She's not going anywhere with you." Miki stepped in front of Sara, but one of the men backhanded her. She flew across the hood of a car, landing on the other side.

A brief moment of silence followed as Sara and Angelina looked over at their fallen friend. Together, they slowly turned back to face the four men standing in front of them.

"Angelina?"

"Yes, Sara?"

Sara stared straight at the leader. "Go," she bit out as her fist slammed into the groin of the man closest to her.

Angelina didn't hesitate. She turned and ran, sliding over the hood of a car and charging flat out back to the hospital.

Sara tore off into the woods. Hoping—praying—they would be more obsessed with getting her then going after Angelina.

She couldn't hear them, but she could smell them. If they shifted she probably didn't stand a chance. She was pretty sure she moved slower as human. And she had no idea how to change to anything. So she ran, and she prayed. Prayed her Pack would come for her before it was too late.

Chapter Nineteen

Zach smelled them before he even hit the parking lot. He, Marrec, and both their Packs already out the door of the hospital when Angelina ran into them. Silently, panic and fear for her friend coming off her in waves, she grabbed Zach by the hand and dragged him to where she last saw Sara.

He caught his female's scent immediately and within seconds shifted, taking off into the woods, shaking his clothes off as he went. His Pack right behind him.

At first, the bastard cats didn't shift. He could still smell the human. Besides, they couldn't taunt and terrify her as cats. Only men could do that. But they must have realized she was a lot faster and stronger than they'd expected. About two miles from the hospital, they changed. And Zach knew it wouldn't be long before they caught up with her. Before they killed her.

He quickly figured out where she was heading. Home. She was going home. To where she felt safe. To where she had guns.

Good girl. Anything she could do at this point to buy him time.

ल्द ल्द ल्द

Sara knew as soon as they shifted, but she kept moving. If she had a moment to think, she would be marveling at the fact she hadn't run since her attack when she was eight. And now she'd run almost five miles and felt—no, she *knew*—she could go another twenty. But they were gaining on her. She'd been right—they were much faster once they shifted.

Sara cleared the woods and made a mad dash for her house. She slid over the hood of a car parked in front of her porch, which bought her precious seconds, flew up the stairs and through her front door. She turned and slammed the door as the cats made it up the stairs. They threw themselves against the wood and she wondered how long before they forced the heavy oak off its hinges. She wondered where Zach and the rest of the Pack were.

She wondered how long before the bitches behind her actually said anything.

Sara looked over her shoulder at the four women standing behind her, one holding her shotgun.

They were beautiful females. Tall. Powerful. Blonde. Really blonde. Impeccably dressed, sporting four-hundred-dollar gold-colored shoes and gold jewelry she could never afford.

"They were right. You do look like your mother."

Talk about having a bad day. Sara sighed and stepped forward to face the leader. She wasn't the tallest, but clearly she ran these females.

"She killed my sister. Now I'm going to kill you," the woman stated simply. "I'd hoped to do it long ago, but that bitch grandmother of yours moved like lightning."

"Then let's end it." Sara was so tired of the bullshit. "Here. Now. Anything to get you to shut the fuck up."

The woman hissed her displeasure and Sara snarled in return, her lips pulling back over her growing canines.

Then the bitch's hand wrapped around Sara's throat, dragging her close. Sara grabbed at the hand cutting off her oxygen as panic swept through her. Panic, fear and anger. Definitely anger. The female leaned in and sniffed her.

"How sweet. Just turned. Just marked." A tongue that should not have been able to fit in the woman's mouth lashed out and swiped up the entire side of Sara's scarred face. It wasn't really wet, but dry and painful where it touched. "I bet he'll miss you when you're gone." Then she lifted Sara off the floor and tossed her across the room and through the closed glass window.

ભ ભ ભ

Zach skid to a halt in front of Sara's porch, Conall practically slamming into the back of him. He watched her body flying toward the window and his mind howled in anger and pain. He was going to lose her. Lose the only woman he liked much less loved. But as Sara's body cleared the glass, he watched her change. Her limbs smoothly shifted to hind and front legs, her hands and feet into paws, black hair spreading over her body. To finish, her beautiful face elongated into a muzzle and snapping jaws.

Then she hit the porch, bounced and flipped off it, sliding across the grass in front of her house and coming to a halt when she slid right into Zach's long front legs.

Like that she'd shifted, officially becoming one of them. One of the Pack. But this was her first shift, and she'd need time to come to terms with it. Time to learn to use her new body. Time none of them had.

Sara felt her body go through the window. Felt the glass shredding her clothes, tearing her flesh. She briefly wondered how long she could fight if she lost a lot of blood.

She hit the porch, bounced once and flipped off it into the air. Then she felt grass and dirt against her body as she slid into Zach. He wasn't the Zach she was used to seeing. He was the wolf she'd set up on her couch. The wolf that possessively watched her from the woods. How did she know the wolf and the man were the same? Easy. She recognized those beautiful eyes. Those beautiful hazel eyes. If she'd seen them last night, she would have known it was him. No one else had eyes like that.

The cats were coming closer. She could smell them and hear them moving, surrounding her and the Pack. Quickly, she scrambled up on all fours, ready to fight.

It took her a good five seconds to realize she was no longer human. She realized she'd shifted when she went through the window. That explained why she'd bounced so easily from the porch. She shook herself out of her clothes as the power of the wolf coursed through her new body. The strength of centuries of breeding and the lust for the hunt and the kill. She turned to the beast behind her father's death. A golden lioness stood on her porch and roared in rage. Sara realized that as a lion, the bitch was huge.

All the cats were. She stared in awe at their size and beauty and tried to figure out how, exactly, she and Zach were going to fight animals weighing a good three-hundred to four-hundred pounds more then any of her Pack did? Then she felt Zach brush up against her. She felt his strength. His power. His utter confidence in her. Confidence in the psychotic bitch he'd come to love.

He was right. She *was* a psychotic bitch. And these heifers had murdered her father. She would probably get herself killed today, but she would hurt, maim and kill as many of them as she possibly could first.

She turned to face them, her lips peeling back to bare her teeth, a snarl angrily forced out of her. And that's when they burst out of the woods—thirty-strong. Marrec and his Pack. People she'd known most of her life. She knew each one even as wolves. Jake. Fogle. Lana from the hair salon, and so many more. She recognized their scent. The rest? True wolves. Wolves and descendents of wolves that had watched over her since she was a child.

Sara turned back to the lioness. Things had just evened up a bit. And being the psychotic bitch she was, she charged her head-on. The lioness let out a roar that shook the trees and went up on her hind legs, but Sara kept coming. She collided with the female, clamping her jaw around the beast's throat. Three of her Pack joined her. Two went for the cat's groin while the other wolf gripped the lion's head in her mouth. They all bit down and wouldn't let go. Even as the lioness fought for her life, Sara still wouldn't release her. Big paws clawed at Sara, tearing her fur-covered flesh. She simply ignored the pain and the blood she felt running down her side and muzzle. Instead she dug her teeth in deeper and, using all her new-found strength, yanked out the bitch's throat. Sara stood back to watch the lioness struggle to get back on her feet. But blood gushed from her wounds and eventually she stopped fighting.

Sara spit out the remains of the lioness and turned to see Zach, Conall and Yates dispatching one male. Marrec and six of his Pack were fighting another. The full-blooded wolves had taken on two male lions. Her Pack had taken on another female.

Two more females came at her, so Sara tore down the steps of her porch and slammed headfirst into one of them. The two bounced off each other into opposite corners. The other lioness was slower and became the tragic victim of a white pickup truck driven by a crazy Latina.

Angelina hit the brakes, violently turning the steering wheel so the truck spun out. The side of the two-ton vehicle hit the lioness and knocked her across the temporary battlefield. Miki leaned out the window, Angelina's shotgun in her hands. Sara watched that expression of cool detachment Miki always got when hunting. Mik pulled the trigger once and the beast gave a pained roar, landing in a heap, a large part of its skull gone. Sara saw that classic Miki smile and knew her friends were as much predators as she was.

Assured her two friends could handle themselves, Sara turned back to see the last female scramble to her big feet. She roared out in anger and frustration. And when she did, Sara attacked, wrapping her maw around the back of the lion's neck and twisting the beast around so they both hit the ground. Then Zach was there beside Sara, grabbing the lion's throat, Conall took hold of the beast's rear right leg. Marrec grabbed the rear left. Casey, Yates and Julie all took a firm grip on exposed flesh. Zach crushed the lion's windpipe and as it struggled to breathe, they all tore her to pieces.

Sara released the animal and trotted over to Miki and Angelina. They looked down at her, but their eyes widened. At first Sara thought they were simply afraid of her as wolf. But she quickly realized she was freezing cold and shaking. Looking down at her crouching form, she saw blood-and-dirt-covered skin. She'd changed back.

"Oh, honey." Angelina reached into the truck and pulled out a blanket.

"I'll take it." Zach, now human, took the blanket and moved toward Sara.

"Dude, some clothes!" Miki, the entire left side of her face already black and blue from the punch, turned away to look at the truck, the ground, anything but her friend's naked boyfriend. Then Miki saw Casey prance by with her muzzle wrapped around a hunk of lion leg. "Okay. You people are killing me!" She rubbed her eyes with balled fists as Angelina put her arm around Miki's shoulders and tried not to laugh.

Zach crouched beside Sara, wrapping the blanket around her.

"Zach, I'm so cold." She barely got that out, her teeth were chattering so hard.

"Don't worry, baby, it's normal. It's your first change. It's to be expected."

Sara still grinned. "My first change? You mean I've popped my change-cherry?"

Zach looked at her and started laughing. "Yeah, I guess you could say that. If you're tacky enough to say that."

He picked Sara up in his arms and held her close, making sure the blanket was tight around her.

"Clothes! You people need clothes!" Sara peeked over Zach's shoulder to see a naked Conall standing behind them and in front of a clearly disturbed Miki. *Considering she's just taken out a three-hundred-pound animal with one shot, you'd think she'd handle the naked thing a little better.*

"Go on," Conall said to Zach. "We'll take care of cleaning this up. You take care of her."

Zach nodded and walked into the house, Sara's head resting against his shoulder.

Within minutes, Zach had Sara in a hot bath. He washed the blood off her face and out of her hair. Cleaned her wounds and gently licked the ones on her neck, face and shoulder. Then he dried her off with a big towel and carried her to bed. Laying down next to her, Zach pulled her to him, resting her head on his chest, his arms tightly wrapped around her long body. He nuzzled her, rubbed his nose against her wet hair and kissed her forehead. Sara sighed once and in a few seconds she was asleep.

It was early morning when she woke him, her naked body stretched out on top of his. Her lips moving along his neck and her hands sliding down his waist.

Zach took her head in his hands and turned her to look at him. To be blunt, she was all fucked up from the previous night's fight—her left eye black and blue, a deep wound on her neck, a vicious cut across the bridge of her nose. *She is so hot,* he thought. And she was glowing. Clearly she took after her mother more than any of them realized. She was all about the hunt.

"Okay, what? What are you staring at? Is there a bug on me?"

He wanted to tell her. Tell her he loved her. Tell her she was his mate and that together they would rule the Magnus Pack. He really wanted to tell her.

"There's something I need to tell you," he finally said and her eyes immediately narrowed with suspicion. "Nothing bad," he added hurriedly. "I don't think."

She pushed herself off him and sat at the other end of the bed. "Well?"

He cleared his throat. "Um...see, after yesterday...you know, you've kind of...well, you've kind of established yourself as the dominant female...which kind of means...that...uh..." She continued to stare at him. Okay. So she wasn't going to make this easy. "You see, it's just that...for the Pack it's all about...um...and for me...you know..." Why was this so hard? Maybe it was the way she watched him, her arms crossed in front of her breasts. "Uh..."

Then her phone went off. Sara held up a finger. "Hold that thought."

She easily swung herself off the bed and grabbed the phone from the top of the TV. "Hello? Hey, Mik. Whasup? You doin' okay? How's your face today?" Sara flopped stomach-down across the bed. Zach stared at that delectable ass and became completely lost, forgetting what he'd been talking about. Who she was talking to. He forgot his own name. He forgot all of it. "Good. Me? I'm doin' just fine. Just waiting for Zach to quit dancin' around the bush and tell me he loves me." Zach was startled but couldn't tear his eyes away from her ass. "Not *that* bush, you perv. Anyway, it's taking him an hour and a day and I'm running out of patience." Sara's legs lazily moved front to back, her breasts barely touching the sheets, her chin tucked into the palm of one hand while the other held the phone to her ear. "That's a good idea. Hold on." She looked at Zach. "Would it help if I told you I loved you first?"

Zach didn't know what to say. Hell, he was still staring at her ass, so he sort of nodded. Sort of.

Sara went back to the phone. "You're right. Apparently that would help. You're so smart." Sara fell silent for a moment, listening to Miki on the other end. "Yeah. You got it." Sara snapped her phone closed and tossed it on the nightstand beside the bed. But she tossed way too hard and the phone hit the wall and flew back, disappearing under the bed. "Well, shit."

Zach watched her lean down to search under the bed. She slid half her body to the floor trying to reach the phone, but all Zach could see was her ass bent over the bed, one leg sliding across his thigh. He growled.

Sara had just gotten her hands on her phone when she felt Zach's tongue slide across her ass. Startled, she flipped off the bed.

Cell phone still gripped in one hand, she pulled herself up to rest on her knees. Zach was laying on the edge of the bed, smirking at her. "Could you warn me before you do something like that?"

"You shake your ass at me like that, you get no warning."

She tried to stop herself from smiling, but simply couldn't. "I'll keep that in mind for the future."

"You mean the future of five seconds from now?" He grabbed her arm and yanked her onto the bed.

"Hey!" Sara's already bruised and damaged face slammed into a pillow. She lifted her head and brushed her hair out of her eyes. "You know, you've been tossing me around a lot."

"Uh-huh." Zach moved up behind her. "And that bothers you because..." He gripped her legs and pulled them apart, then dragged her down until her ass was on his lap.

"I didn't say it bothered me, I just think I deserve a little more respect than that. You know, with me being Alpha Female and all." His head snapped up in surprise and she grinned at him. "Don't look so surprised. I'm not stupid. I knew in the hospital, when you wanted me to yell at the girls. Hey!" she yelped when he slapped her ass.

"You're a real smart ass, you know that? But I'll let it go because you have such an amazing butt." As if to prove it, he slapped her ass again.

She growled. "You know, I'm not your..." She stopped and they looked at each other. They both knew what the next word out of her mouth was going to be. "Okay. So maybe I am your bitch, that doesn't mean I'm your chew toy."

Zach raised one eyebrow, and Sara watched him lean down and lick her lower back. Her hands gripped the sheets. "You asshole, you're trying to distract me again." His tongue took its time moving across her hot and hungry flesh and it felt so good, she wasn't sure what the hell she'd been complaining about.

"What were you saying, beautiful?" he asked as she felt his thick fingers slowly entering her pussy, his tongue lapping at her accursed damaged thigh. Sheets shredded under her hands as she looked back at him. And there was that smug prick she'd grudgingly fallen in love with. The wounds he'd sustained on his face, neck, chest and back the night before had already begun to heal. He'd gotten every one of those rips and tears because of her and he didn't care. She knew he didn't care. Clearly the only thing Zach Sheridan cared about at the moment was getting her wet and getting her off.

He caught her staring at him and nipped her ass cheek. "What ya starin' at?" he demanded playfully.

But her reply was deadly serious. "You. I love you, Zach."

He looked at her for several moments then leaned down and kissed her ass. His hands slid under her breasts and, holding them firmly but gently, lifted her so that her back was flat against his chest.

Kissing her along her neck and shoulder, he stopped to lick wounds new and old. When he reached her ear, he leaned in closer than anyone before him ever had. "I love you, baby," he whispered. "More than anything." Then he was inside her and she forgot about everything else.

Chapter Twenty

Miki held up a tennis ball, looked at Sara's new Pack, and tossed it out into the forest away from the ongoing rave. They all watched it go, then they turned back to Miki.

"Okay. Go—"

Sara and Angelina slapped their hands over Miki's mouth before the word "fetch" could come out of it.

They pulled her over to one of the food tables.

"*Are you out of your ever-loving mind?* Everyone here *but us* is like Sara," Angelina snarled. "And after seeing them in action I'd rather not fuck with them!"

Miki gave that innocent smile. "It was just a little experiment."

"I don't want to know."

How sweet. Her friends were having one last fight before she left. Tomorrow she'd leave with Zach. Back to her original home with the man she loved. She wasn't sure, but she thought her father would be happy about that. She knew her grandmother wouldn't be. That thought made her giddy.

The last thing they were doing before they left was throw this all-night rave for Marrec and his Pack. Seemed only fair after they helped her tear a whole Pride to pieces.

But the mere thought of leaving was sending her into a full-blown panic attack. How was she going to leave her best friends? These crazy bitches had risked their lives for her, accepted her for who and what she was, and were there whenever she needed them. She knew she should tell them that. She knew she should tell them how much she loved them. Instead she turned to Angelina and glanced down at the four-hundred dollar shoes on her friend's feet. Sara raised one eyebrow and grinned. "Those are nice gold-colored shoes, Santiago."

"Actually they're champagne. My signature color. They look fabulous on me, don't they? I just found them...ya know...lying around."

Sara tried to think how she was going to do any of this without these two. Already the females of the Pack were waiting for Sara to give them orders. She didn't know what to tell them, although "Move out of my way" seemed to be quite effective at the moment. And thankfully she knew music and DJs because apparently she was partnering with Zach to take over the club business from Yates and Casey. Considering she had no idea what she would do with the rest of her life just the week before, it was kind of startling to suddenly be "in charge" of anything. Especially a thriving business. She didn't want to disappoint them or Zach. She especially didn't want to disappoint herself. Deep down she knew she could do it. Unfortunately that knowledge didn't stop the panic from causing her to hyperventilate in the bathroom just ten minutes before.

Then again maybe she couldn't do this. Maybe she shouldn't leave. Just because she could suddenly shift into a wolf at will didn't mean she should leave what she knew best. It definitely didn't mean she should change her whole life for some guy she just met. Hell, they hadn't even gone on an actual date. Christ, did wolves date? And if they did date where did they go? To dinner at a restaurant or hunting down some deer? Nope. Nope. She couldn't do this. She was nobody's Alpha Female. She'd have to tell Zach to forget it. He could just take his big cock and go. Yup, that was the plan. Good plan.

That's how it started in the bathroom, too, and in a few more seconds the hyperventilating would begin again...

Zach's big arms snaked around her body from behind. He kissed her neck and pulled her close against him and, suddenly, it all felt right. *He* felt right. Him and his big cock.

"Ladies." He nodded at her two friends. "Hope you're having a good time."

They both grinned in return, momentarily distracted from the oncoming slap fight.

"Great little party," Angelina offered with one of her dazzling smiles.

"Thanks." He snuggled closer to Sara. "Dance. Eat. Everything's on the house for you two." He paused. "But please don't ask our Pack to fetch anymore."

Sara and Angelina cringed as Miki rolled her eyes. "It was just an experiment. Honestly."

She turned to walk away but crashed into her own personal shapeshifting stalker.

"Hey, Miki." Conall smiled. "I think you dropped this." He handed Miki the tennis ball.

"Dude!" Zach barked.

"What?"

Zach gave a brutal snort of disgust and walked away.

They were polite enough to wait until Conall followed after his friend, asking Zach to tell him what he did wrong, before the three friends burst out laughing.

"No one is safe around you three."

Sara turned to find Marrec behind her. She threw her arms around his neck and hugged him tight. "Thank you so much, Marrec. Thank you for everything." And she wasn't only talking about the fight with the Pride. She was talking about the last twenty years.

"You're welcome. But are you trying to get me killed?"

Sara opened her eyes and saw Zach watching her from fifty feet away. He definitely didn't seem too pleased. "Or maybe you're trying to get yourself killed?" Sara looked and saw Marrec's wife glaring at her. Funny, the woman had made her graduation dress and had always invited her to every Marrec family event. Now she acted as if Sara were some hooker on the street trying to pick up her husband.

Sara pulled away and looked at Marrec. "I can never come back here, can I?"

"Sara, you'll always be welcome here. But never as Alpha Female."

Sara gave a half-smile. "So I can never come back here, can I?"

Marrec smiled like a proud father. "That's my girl."

She stepped away from him. "Have a great time tonight. Everything is free for you and your Pack. Enjoy."

"We will." He turned to head back to his mate.

"I'll miss you," she whispered, knowing he would hear her. He nodded once and walked away.

"Are you okay?" Angelina put her hand on her friend's shoulder. All three of them had been close to Marrec, for varying reasons he was the only father they'd ever really known.

Sara took a deep breath. "Yeah. I'll be okay." She was feeling such a huge sense of loss she wondered how she could face the rest of the night.

Miki appeared at Sara's elbow but she glared at Angelina. "You know, I wasn't doing anything wrong." Apparently she had been arguing with

Angelina in her head for the last ten minutes. "Just seeing what their play-drive is like. That Conall guy clearly has a big play-drive."

"They're not dogs, you idiot."

"Um...I know you didn't just call me an idiot."

"Um..." Angelina imitated back, "I think I just did."

Yup. There went that sense of loss. Sara realized when she left the next morning there would be no tearful goodbyes with these two. This wasn't goodbye. These crazy women would always be her best friends. Besides, you never get rid of friends like these. They follow you to hell so they can torture you for eternity.

When Angelina poked Miki in the shoulder with one manicured fingernail, Sara left. Zach had disappeared, but she followed his scent into the woods.

ભ ભ ભ

Zach leaned against a tree. He was about half a mile away from the rave, waiting for Sara. And he knew she'd find him.

He smelled her lust even before he heard her. Shit. His dick went hard again.

"You runnin' away from me already?" Now that she'd healed and become what she was always meant to be, Sara moved with a grace and power he found amazing. She was truly becoming the ultimate she-wolf and loving every minute of it.

"Nope. Just trying to figure out how I could live in California all my life and never once say 'dude'. But after hanging out with you three bitches for five days, I suddenly sound like an idiot."

She punched him in the shoulder. "Dude. That's harsh."

Sara grinned and Zach rubbed his eyes with his palms. "You're going to make me crazy."

"It's a gift."

He decided to change the subject. "Your friends arguing, how long will that be going on anyway?"

"Finger pointing just started. Next there'll be yelling. Then, depending how bad it gets, a good old-fashioned slap fight. So it could take hours."

Her friends were definitely crazier than she was, but only marginally. "Interesting. Any nudity involved?"

Sara nuzzled him under his chin and Zach leaned in and smelled the fresh scent of her hair. "Sorry, mister. No other bitches for you. You're stuck with just me. Golden Retriever Sara."

He laughed. "Who?"

She kissed him. "Forget it."

"Gladly." He ran his hand across the scarred side of her face. She didn't flinch away, but instead leaned into it. "You're sure about this, right?" He'd never asked her if she wanted to go home with him. He'd assumed, but he was starting to realize assuming anything with this woman was a bad move.

"I don't know. California. Actors. Hollywood." She stuck her tongue out. "Yuck."

"Don't stick that thing out unless you plan to use it. And it's Northern California. Completely different from Southern California. Worlds apart. Besides, you were born there. Not here."

"I may not have been born here, but I was made here. And don't you forget it."

"Is that a yes or a no?"

Busy sliding her hands under his T-shirt and running her fingers over his abs, Sara wasn't remotely paying attention. "About what?"

He sighed—deeply—and for some unknown reason that seemed to make her chuckle.

"Are you coming with me?"

"Sure. But on one condition."

Zach closed his eyes. "It involves *them* doesn't it?"

"They're my family. So that means every Thanksgiving, Christmas, New Years, Fourth of July, and because Angelina's Catholic, Easter. You attend dinner and you're cheery."

"I'm never cheery," he stated flatly. And honestly.

"But for me, you will be."

He shook his head in resignation. "Fine. Whatever."

"Good. Then yes, I'm coming with you." She grabbed his hand and began to pull him back to the rave. "Now, feed me, wolf. Your mate's starving."

"Sara. Wait." He stopped walking and tugged on her hand. "I think they want to say goodbye."

Sara frowned as he motioned toward the forest. A female, the Alpha of the full wolves, walked into the pale light cast from the rave. Her Pack stood behind her, the dozen pairs of eyes watching Zach closely. They still weren't sure he was good enough for Sara. He smiled. Without even trying, Sara earned a loyalty from man and beast he'd never seen before.

The female brushed against Sara, her big body pushing against Sara's legs. She circled them once and returned to her Pack. Zach waited for them to leave, move on silently into the night, but the female had one more thing she had to do before she could let Sara go.

The she-wolf tilted her head back and howled, her Pack joining in. But when the Packs at the rave howled back, both Zach and Sara exchanged startled glances.

"I've never seen anything like this before," Zach whispered in awe as the howling continued. "Three Packs." He ran his hand down Sara's back. "Three Packs howling to you, baby."

Sara turned and looked at her mate, a frown flitting across her beautiful features as recognition dawned. "It was you the other night, wasn't it?" she asked quietly as she brushed his hair out of his eyes. "That howling I heard that wasn't like the others. The one I felt..." She closed her eyes for a moment, the memory washing over her. "It was you," she repeated as her gaze again focused on him. "You called to me."

Zach didn't reply. He didn't have to. She already knew the answer. Instead he gripped his mate tight around her hips, pulling her into him. Sara nuzzled her face against his as she trapped him against the tree with her long body.

"I thought you wanted to go eat?" he growled low as her hands moved down his body. A few more inches and she wasn't going anywhere anytime soon.

"You better fuck me first, wolf." She unzipped his jeans and slid her hand inside. "Your mate's starving."

He's a shape-shifting wolf, she's a psychic and his other half. In order to catch a killer, Caelen has to rely on his Seeing Eye Mate. Coming to Samhain Publishing October 24, 2006.

Enjoy this excerpt from

Seeing Eye Mate

(c)2006 Annmarie McKenna

"Get away from the window, my mate."

"You know, we really need to talk about that," she muttered, ignoring his softly issued command. "This is the weirdest thing. There are these two dogs—"

Her feet flew out from under her, making her tummy flip as she went down beneath Caelan's crushing weight. His arms wrapped around her, protecting her from what should have been a rough landing and she fought to catch her breath through her squished lungs.

"They're just dogs, Cael, it's fine," Eli announced.

Tieran blinked slowly, trying to refocus on her upside-down world. Eli was staring out the window and Caelan's chest vibrated along her arm with his fierce growling. He nuzzled her throat to a more open position and his sharp teeth rasped along her neck.

She jerked her head away, suddenly very aware of her surroundings. Who wouldn't be when their lover was planting more than a love bite at a very vulnerable spot?

"Ouch, get off me." She squirmed and tried to dislodge him but instead the action caused him to bite down harder. When she stilled, his jaws loosened. Her pulse beat a wild tattoo just below where his tongue lapped at her neck.

"Caelan!" Tieran wiggled again, he bit her again. Any harder and he'd puncture her jugular, she thought wildly. She submitted, giving him what he obviously wanted.

Submission? Bullshit. She'd turn into the tooth fairy before she submitted to him.

"Yet there you are, laying so still beneath your wolf-man, Tulla."

Ah hell. Her gramama was right.

Her lungs deflated on a huge sigh. Above them, Eli chuckled. Finally the razor sharp teeth were removed from her skin.

"The next time I tell you to fucking do something, by God, you better do it." Caelan's growl was laced with deadly menace in her ear, but she detected something else too. Nervousness? Anxiousness?

His tongue flicked out, lapping at the wound he'd inflicted, making her forget everything. He smelled so good. Like sweat and man and sex from their earlier romp. She looped an ankle around his calf and pulled his leg between hers, fitting his thigh snugly against her pussy. Finally! Maybe she could relieve some of the tension that throbbed at her clit.

"Mmm." She wrapped her free hand around the back of his scalp and angled her head to give him better access. Not that he needed it. He was doing just fine on his own.

His mouth moved to her earlobe and sucked it deep. She imagined it was her nipple he had embedded in that wet heat. She wanted his hands on her. Wanted to feel him tugging and pinching the sensitive beads. She lifted her hips and rubbed herself on his thigh. It wasn't enough! There were too many clothes in the way. She needed his fingers, his tongue, or better yet his cock, inside her, filling her. Not where it was, poking into her side.

"Man, you guys are hot."

"Oh shit." Tieran yanked herself free from Caelan and raised up on her elbows, her chest heaving with each breath. What in the hell was happening to her? She'd certainly liked having sex before, but until now, having it wasn't a requirement. Not a need that festered like an infected wound. She'd never craved it like she did with Caelan. And she'd never lost control in a way that everything around her disappeared.

Her cheeks flamed. Eli stood above them, watching as she and his brother went at it on her living room floor like two randy teenagers.

ର ର ର

Caelan couldn't resist smiling as he rolled more firmly on his side and propped his head on his hand. He reached out and palmed the small cotton-covered breast furthest from him, flicking at the nipple. If Eli hadn't interrupted—for Tieran's sake, 'cause it damned well wasn't for his—Caelan would have fucked her right here on the hardwood floor.

"Stop it." Tieran slapped at his hand. "Your brother is watching."

He shrugged. "So?"

Her eyes widened, her face drained of color, and she gulped. "Please don't tell me you guys do that...that...sharing stuff," she hissed.

Caelan snarled; Eli burst out laughing.

"Nobody but me will ever touch you," Caelan growled.

"Sweetheart, I'm not ready to die." Eli reached a hand down and pulled Caelan to his feet.

"What does that mean?"

"Wolves mate for life." Caelan winced at his gruff attitude, but goddamn, share her? Never. He helped her off the floor and guided her to the sofa. He needed to sit and have a drink after nearly having his heart ripped out. When she'd said dogs, he immediately assumed she wasn't looking at dogs, but wolves. Rogue wolves on the prowl and looking for another kill.

Eli scratched his head and sat across from them. "What it really means is that as a Prime's mate, you are the alpha bitch. The only way I'll *ever* get to touch you, is for me to fight Caelan to the death and take over the pack. I'm really not all that intrigued by the prospect."

Tieran turned away from Eli. "Did he just call me a bitch? 'Cause I really don't think he's known me long enough to make that kind of presumption."

Caelan choked on his mouthful of beer, spitting it across the room. "Only you," he said when he could breathe again, "could make that kind of statement and totally ignore the part about him killing me." He threaded his fingers through hers and gathered her closer until she was tucked under his arm.

Introducing Rene Lyons with an excerpt from her sexy and enthralling vampire romance, Midnight Sun. Where the damned come to play...

Enjoy this excerpt from

Midnight Sun

(c) 2006 Rene Lyons

"Where is she?"

Constantine's demand held a note of accusation Sebastian didn't care for in the least. If Allie weren't still here he'd beat the Dragon senseless for the implication in his tone.

Biting back his indignation, he motioned to the bathroom door. "In there."

"In one piece?"

"Bloody hell!" Sebastian stood and strode over to the fireplace. He slapped his palms again the black granite mantle in a rare burst of emotion. "Of course in one piece, you bloody bastard."

ᘒ ᘒ ᘒ

Allie's body might be intact, but her mind was shattered into a million pieces.

Good God, the man can kiss!

Needing to clear her head, she splashed cold water on her face. Sebastian's kiss left her as close to drunk as she'd ever come. He worked her mouth with the expertise of a man who had centuries to perfect his form.

Pulling down her bottom lip, she saw a nice gash. He caught her good with those razor sharp fangs of his. Amazingly, she hadn't even felt it happen.

Letting go of her lip, she dismissed the cut, assuming accidents were bound to happen when you had fangs hanging out of your mouth.

A wonderful shiver passed through her, as she wished she were still lost in his kiss. His raw masculinity woke everything feminine in her. He was all grace and beauty, with a deadly ferocity simmering under the cool façade he presented to the world.

After tasting a small sample of Sebastian's fire, Allie was left shaken and wanting more. Not even Jude, a handsome man in his own way, moved her as Sebastian did.

What a shame it wasn't going to go much beyond this kiss.

Though embroiled in the same nocturnal world, they walked vastly different roads. Allie couldn't imagine the two of them mixing well together since he was of the dead and she of the living. It might work with just a friendship, as it did with Constantine and Raphael, but anything more could end in a huge mess, leaving her with a broken heart.

Though if a woman was to have her heart broken, she could do worse than a man as sexy and mysterious as Sebastian.

Ripped with thick cords of muscle, he oozed strength and sex appeal. Everything about him appealed to her, from his shorn head to the dragon tattoo on his upper arm. He was sexy as hell and it drove her insane how he pointedly ignored her when all she wanted to do was rip his clothes off.

As someone who was tattooed herself, she was dying to get a good look at the dragon piece that covered his upper arm and some of his neck. She doubted she'd ever get the chance unless she tied him down and had her way with him.

Not a bad idea if I do say so myself.

Turning off the water, she heard Raphael's voice coming from the bedroom. Quitting the black marble bathroom, Allie threw open the door that connected to Sebastian's room and waved at her friends.

"Hey guys. Here." Fishing around in her pocket, she pulled out Raphael's key and handed it to him.

At the same moment, Constantine's gaze shot to her bottom lip. He sniffed at the air, a vicious snarl curling back his upper lip. "Why the fuck is she bleeding?"

Unfazed by Constantine's furious demand, Sebastian threw him a glare. Before things got out of hand, as it easily could when dealing with vampires, Allie waved a hand through the air dismissively. "It's nothing. We were making with the nice-nice and Sebastian's fang accidentally caught my lip."

Three male jaws practically hit the floor when she carelessly threw out that tidbit.

Oblivious to the murderous glares Raphael and Constantine were directing at Sebastian, she turned around and glanced in the mirror hanging over the black lacquer dresser. "See? The bleeding already stopped."

Turning back, she finally noted how furious her friends were. Obviously it didn't seem to matter that he clipped her by accident. By their reaction one would think he tore off a chuck of her lip and was still gnawing on it when they burst in on him.

She also noticed Sebastian looked like he wanted to wring her neck.

Raphael was the first to snap out of his stupor at her flippancy. Given that his anger was now directed at her, Allie wished he was still struck dumb.

"I've known you for five months and not once did you '*make with the nice-nice*' with me. You're around Sebastian for five minutes and you're making out with him."

Allie rolled her eyes over his argument. "Don't go getting your panties in a bunch about it. Just because I never swooned at your feet when you tried those ridiculous lines on me doesn't mean I was immune to you. Jeez, Raphael, look at yourself! You're gorgeous. How could I not be attracted to you? But you're my friend. And I don't know," she shrugged, "I don't see you in a sexual way."

Constantine raised a brow at her. "So what am I? Dog shit?"

Allie closed her eyes and pressed her fingers to her temple in exasperation. "I am not having this conversation."

When she opened her eyes, she saw Sebastian casually leaning his hip against the fireplace looking entirely too amused. "This is all your fault."

He stabbed a finger at his chest and shot his brows up in askance. "Me? How the hell am I at fault here?"

Her hands going to her hips, she matched the glare he was giving her with one of her own. "If you didn't go and kiss me, I wouldn't have kissed you back and I wouldn't have to try to convince two furious vampires that I think they're hot."

She went to storm out, but Sebastian prevented her dramatic exit when he moved with the speed of lightening and grabbed her. Again.

"Allie," he said too calmly. "Did it ever occur to you that those two," he motioned to Constantine and Raphael, "wanted us to get together?"

Why would it take her friends this long to work their scheme if they could have executed it months ago? Ready to dismiss Sebastian's presumption, she peered over his shoulder to see two guilty-looking vampires suddenly vastly interested in the dark gray rug.

"They knew I was going to be home tonight."

Allie laughed at how guilty they looked—even Constantine—which shocked the hell out of her. "You sly dogs."

Yanking her arm from Sebastian's grasp, she went over to Constantine, giving him a good shot to the arm. "I didn't even see this coming."

"That's because you're too damn trusting."

"Maybe," she retorted with a shrug. "I gotta go. You guys can deal with Sebastian's anger on your own. I'll see you tomorrow night."

Unbeknownst to her, three men watched intently as she flounced from the room.

CR CR CR

Once she left, Raphael looked to Sebastian. "Well Sage, how pissed are you?"

Sebastian ignored him, instead going after Allie. Constantine let out a grunt of satisfaction. "Something tells me he's not half as pissed as he wants us to believe."

Raphael slipped him a sly grin. "Think if we bother him enough about it he'll tell us all the juicy details?"

Constantine shrugged. "Doubt it, but I'll see if I can get into his head and find out."

CR CR CR

"Wait." Sebastian called to Allie.

She froze and turned on the darkened steps. "What is it?"

With the night wrapped around her, she looked vulnerable swallowed by the shadows of the staircase. "I don't want you to leave thinking I was sorry for what passed between us."

The emerald fire in her eyes nearly scorched him. "Don't worry. I don't."

"Good," he said gruffly. His body reacted violently when he saw her lick her lips. Thoughts he had no business entertaining about exactly what he wanted her to do with her tongue—and lips and teeth—hardened his body painfully.

The quick, yet infinitely tender kiss she placed on his lips squeezed at his dead heart. Reminding him what it felt like to beat with life, he'd never missed being alive as much as did then.

"Good night, Sebastian."

This time, when she turned to leave he let her go. Unable to move, to speak, he was struck dumb by the wealth of affection he felt in the gentle touch of her lips. He knew only one thing for certain right at that moment—now that he tasted her passion and affection, he wasn't going to let her get away.

Not when her kiss gave the promise of life denied him for seven hundred years.

Samhain Publishing, Ltd.

It's all about the story…

Action/Adventure
Fantasy
Historical
Horror
Mainstream
Mystery/Suspense
Non-Fiction
Paranormal
Red Hots!
Romance
Science Fiction
Western
Young Adult

http://www.samhainpublishing.com